HARRIS PUBLIC LIBRARY

HOURS OF OPENING:—
MONDAY, TUESDAY, WED. & FRIDAY—10 a.m.—8 p.m.
THURSDAY & SATURDAY—10 a.m.—5 p.m.

DATE OF RETURN	DATE OF RETURN	DATE OF RETURN

W. 20M 7

D1135549

XG

THE GREAT FLOOD

Also by Louise Collis

*

Novels:
WITHOUT A VOICE
A YEAR PASSED
AFTER THE HOLIDAY
THE ANGEL'S NAME

Historical Essays:
SEVEN IN THE TOWER

Biographies:
THE APPRENTICE SAINT
SOLDIER IN PARADISE

The Great Flood

LOUISE COLLIS

MACMILLAN

London · Melbourne · Toronto

1966

MACMILLAN AND COMPANY LIMITED
Little Essex Street London WC 2
also Bombay Calcutta Madras Melbourne

THE MACMILLAN COMPANY OF CANADA LIMITED
70 Bond Street Toronto 2

PRINTED IN GREAT BRITAIN

I

Joseph Platt jumped off the train and scuttled down the stairs. 'Home at last,' he whispered. 'How I love the dark, the rain, the anonymity of all these people hurrying through the subway like leaves before a gale. How the damp smells welcome me as if I'd been away a lifetime instead of thirteen hours.' He emerged into the station yard as the crowd began running for their cars, passing swiftly through the lighted patches made by several lamps. He stood watching, and some who knew him by repute, or sight, paused also, curiously regarding his absorbed, excited face on which the glasses flashed like jewels with every movement of his head. They did not, however, accost him. Something in his dream forbade it.

'Now when the shadows of the night are down,' he muttered while a sensuous joy pervaded him, 'I can get started. I can get to grips with it. I feel strong enough to put aside the rubbish I've been talking the whole day. Oh, the lies, the nonsense and, what's more, the positive betrayal, darling, of everything that happened in those times. You see, the trouble is that I say whatever the person I'm with wants to hear, because it makes me more interesting. Because I have a fatal knack of twisting round the truth. Holding it up in the air, you know, like a sparkling silver ball and twirling it in conjurer's hands till everyone applauds. Clap-clap, clap. Laughter. Admiration. Sympathy. I can't resist. I don't try. On the contrary, inspira-

1

tion floods my brain, comes pouring over my tongue and out between my teeth. Heaven knows what I actually say. I can't remember afterwards — not the very words, that is, only the gist of it, the marvellous shining gist.'

He stepped out into the empty yard. Not one traveller had been left behind. Rain poured down and all the lamps shimmered on the pools, the rivulets, cascades and little waterfalls that tumbled from the gutter pipes and played a dancing tune as background to his thoughts, which seemed intensified and polished by the wet, so swiftly and so neatly did they scurry through his mind. Everything was magnified by multiple reflection. The clocktower loomed immensely tall. The station up above on the embankment was a pavilion on a cliff. Those two figures gesticulating in an upstairs room could not possibly be real. He stopped for a moment with his mouth open.

'You see the difficulty, darling,' he muttered earnestly, hurrying on again. 'One should be scientific and conduct experiments to decide whether it is all true; or none of it; or whether, as is perhaps more likely on the whole, one suffers from hallucinations. But hallucinations are a fact of life, as well-attested as anything else. They're great fun, too,' he muttered, slackening pace. 'The days would be horribly dull without them.' He paused to watch three screws of paper bobbing and twirling past his feet. Suddenly, they jumped into a drain. He looked down the grating and could see no sign.

Now a great sense of urgency possessed him. 'There's so much left to do,' he cried, flying over streets and pavements, drops spraying from his coat. 'I've let myself float round and round in dreams and makebelieve. Theatricals, to be precise, have occupied my life. What a waste. It has always been my intention to make a mark.' He gestured on the air. 'To be remembered — in a small way, naturally —

2

by posterity. But for that much work and concentrated thought are necessary,' he sighed. 'I wonder whether I'm sufficiently industrious. It's hard to understand how years can pass so quickly, gone before one has had time to do the many things one planned.'

He saw his house, a dark space between illuminated neighbours at the bottom of the road. No one had opened the gate, he found. The latch was tied up still. No shoes, or boots, had trodden on his weed-grown path. No hand had hammered on the door, thank God. With some assurance, therefore, he slid the key into the lock and turned it. This was the supreme moment of his day.

'Sweetheart!' he said in a suffocated voice. 'Here we are again, at last. You can't imagine how I've longed ... how agitated ... my expectations and my memories all gloriously mixed up.'

So exclaiming, he rushed through six or seven vacant rooms, not stopping till he reached the one he lived in. It contained a single bed; a broken sofa; five shelves with far more volumes on them than were comfortable; an open cupboard spilling notebooks, pads and miscellaneous papers in profusion; a table on which a typewriter lay buried under open books and books with many markers in them and sheets of manuscript closely written, scarcely altered anywhere.

He shut the door with a voluptuous sigh, lit the fire and took a towel from under the bed to dry his hair.

2

THE next morning it was still raining as hard as ever.
Joseph listened to it as he lay in bed. Many of the gutters
round his roof were blocked, causing waterspouts to form
at various points. He heard them plunging into the
tangled bushes below. Often, in the spring particularly, he
thought of going out with sickles, knives, clippers,
choppers and demolishing some of this undergrowth. It
would be rather nice to visit the bottom of the garden, he
sometimes felt, to stroll along the old brick path and
examine the shed at the end of it. There were many
memories, as well as other objects, in that place.

He had the necessary implements stacked in the outside
lavatory, where he handled them occasionally and wiped
off a little rust with the paper. But he had never even cut
the nearest nettles, let alone the laurels, hollies, privets,
syringas, hawthorns grown together in a barricade. Beyond
was the great mound of brambles under which the shed
had completely disappeared. The best view of it could be
obtained from the boxroom window. At certain times of
the year—generally the autumn—he would ascend the
attic stairs at dusk and climb over the boxes, trunks,
packing-cases, chests of drawers, open the window and lean
out, slowly passing his tongue over his lips. Meanwhile, a
very lovely warm feeling crept up and down his skin.

Enough of that! He sprang from the bed and seized his
clothes. 'You see, the thing is,' he whispered, rapidly button-

ing, 'that I daren't delay any longer. I have such night-mares. I lose my appetite and other symptoms, too numer-ous to mention, afflict me daily. Perhaps I ought to consult someone. A professional opinion would be reassuring. It might prove me wrong in my own diagnosis. But that's impossible, he laughed. Oh, quite. Why, I've been arguing for twenty years without a sign of a solution. The subject is still just as fascinating as it was on the first day, the first page, in that notebook up there.'

He stood on the arm of the sofa and stretched to the top shelf in the cupboard, eventually extracting a green Wool-worth exercise book. The cover had been too much fingered already and the corners were turned up. He opened it, but did not read any of the pale spidery writing that ran from leaf to leaf without the slightest inter-mission. In some places the letters were rather large; in others, very small and bolting. It gave the impression of having been composed during a single night of great emotion. This was so.

Determined to procrastinate no further, he got off the sofa, hardly glancing out into the street along which a vast procession of umbrellas was passing. He could just perceive innumerable feet moving in and out beneath them. Efficiency, efficiency, he vowed, tumbling down the stairs, snatching up the letters off the mat, putting on the kettle, planking bread and butter, marmalade upon the table. Was there one more clean plate? He'd read the corre-spondence while the tea was brewing. The answers, where necessary, could be dealt with as he ate. He kept pens, pads, envelopes, stamps, ready everywhere, even in those parts of the house he did not often visit for reasons he hoped fully to explain one day, if time were granted.

The first letter stated: Dear Mr Platt, Being a great admirer of your work, I have elected to make it the subject of a thesis for the Diploma in Creative Writing I am to take next year. As I see it, you are one of the seminal writers of our age. Nowhere is the commitment to the problems of our predicament more total than in the pages of your books. These self-evident facts have not yet been properly appreciated by the critics, as I believe. I should like also to trace throughout the influence on you of Kafka, Dostoevsky, d'Annunzio and Gide.

An ambiguous smile settled itself on Joseph's face as he read on through several more pages of this rubbish. Here was the culmination of his many years' apprenticeship, during which an unremitting poverty had nurtured such a taste for the simple life, such an affection for dismal surroundings, that no one now would take him, at first sight, for a man quite free of financial worry. He had difficulty in believing it himself and always put off paying bills until the third, or fourth, demand from plain dread of writing cheques.

Begging letters gave him a curious sensation. His present correspondent, in most respectful language, it was true, required a photograph, two copies of each of his works and answers to a long list of questions and conundrums, some distinctly on the impertinent side. Was he married? How many times? What were the details? Had any of his family ever suffered from fits? There seemed to be a definite acquaintance with them in one of his earlier novels. Or drink? Or mental disturbances, to be listed under *a*, *b*, *c*, *d*, etc., for the sake of clarity? Many of the greatest geniuses had had to surmount similar obstacles and these had proved a spur to, rather than a millstone round, their gifts. It was desirable to include in the thesis a disquisition on such points in order to render it exhaustive and likely to obtain for its author the coveted Diploma in Creative Writing.

Joseph found himself unable any longer to fix his attention on the letter, or perhaps petition was a more appropriate word. It seemed to mumble on and on like someone in delirium. He put it in the wastepaper basket, of which he kept several in every room. The kitchen ones were all full. Only by stamping on the top was it possible to make sufficient space for new detritus.

The other letter was mercifully short. It said: Sir, Unless the enclosed account is settled within seven days, we shall be regretfully obliged to institute proceedings against you. This he impaled on a spike beside the draining board.

Now it was impossible to delay longer. Not only that, but it would be sinful, having regard to the inexorable passage of time. Tick-tock-tick. He placed the breakfast things in the sink and tore upstairs, muttering, 'Darling, darling, how on earth have so many years evaporated, leaving no trace except a greater accumulation of unsatisfactory notes, drafts, and those sustained, essentially deceitful flights, my published books? And a number of grey hairs,' he added, leaning on the mantelpiece, his nose practically touching the looking-glass. He could also see the window, obliquely reflected, and a gleaming band of umbrellas jogging across the bottom pane.

He thought of opening the window and addressing the people, shouting: Listen, listen, listen! This is the veritable truth. I swear it. You shall have ways of checking it independently of what I say. I shall provide them. Nothing could be easier. It's the sensation of the town, the year, the age — what am I saying? Help me, that's what I mean. Save me. Come into this room and drag me out of it by force. Burn the place and then perhaps, at last, I shall be free. All the umbrellas would halt and tip back and he would see the white faces underneath them, staring up.

Instead, he took his pen and, sitting calmly down, began to write.

7

3

LET'S go back, sweetheart, to the day we met. It's always best to start at the beginning and work on from there, refusing to be distracted by future events until one comes to them. Not that such a course is as easily pursued as you might think. Far from it. I believe several hundredweights of false starts must be lying round about me now. That's how one's time and energy are stolen away for ever. Your time and mine. On that first day I had absolutely no inkling that we were to embark on a lifelong struggle.

I turned into the bottom of the street and saw you, facing inwards, half-way up. It was a beautiful spring afternoon and the sun shone gloriously, but was prevented by the height of the buildings from reaching the shadows where we stood. Other people hurried along the pavement. You remained quite still while I approached as quickly as I could, in case your dream should slacken and you be gone, round some corner, through some door, before I reached the spot. I did not pause to consider why I had this great desire to meet you, because that would have been fatal. The pros and cons, the adding up, the second thoughts and memories of past encounters of a similar sort would have taken far too long.

I was therefore a little breathless as I finally stopped beside you, noting that your attention was entirely fixed on a window above which was written, in illuminated letters, Ladies' Turkish Bath. It was impossible to see into the

8

building, on account of an arrangement of mirrors, cut in fancy Turkish shapes and concealing the interior. The glass door was similarly obscured. It was certainly possible to imagine that the place was full of naked ladies, lobster-coloured, baking, steaming, dousing, drying, but there were no definite signs that this was, in fact, the case. On the contrary, the steps looked dusty and the door fast shut for ever.

I stood slightly behind you. We were both reflected in the Turkish mirrors which, I now observed, had brown spots all over them and one or two chips round the edges. But what really struck me was your amazing pallor, as if you suffered from anaemia, or severe nervous strain. This decided me to speak. For I could still have got away. You hadn't seen me standing by you in the glass.

'Madam,' I said softly, unobtrusively, 'these baths have closed. I have had prior information of it. The machinery broke down and the lease was too short to make repairs worth while. Spare parts for Turkish baths are not easily obtained and the necessary workmen are expensive to engage.'

Turning on me the strangest pair of light-green eyes I ever saw, you replied, 'What's that you say?'

'I say that these baths have been bought up by a betting combine,' I cried with the utmost enthusiasm. 'Next month they are to be demolished and modern premises, replete with every convenience, erected in their place. One will be able to place bets even on quite insignificant races, or prize fights, in China.'

'Indeed,' you said politely, leaning against an adjacent set of railings with remarkable elegance, or so it seemed to me. I was more and more convinced, darling, that this so-called chance meeting was of supreme importance. I felt already that there was something extraordinary between

9

us. The sun was now receding up the walls of these enormous houses, leaving us together in a cool grey cleft.

'Many titled ladies have patronized these baths,' I continued in a rapid voice, fearing you might depart. 'I am a journalist and have contributed to gossip columns on the subject. I had an assistant, naturally, to go in and collect the copy. Though very hideous, she had a photographic memory which was invaluable. For, of course, notebooks and pencils were out of the question in that atmosphere and she had nowhere to conceal the bijou recording machine so useful at parties, weddings, nightclubs and other low dives sometimes fancied by the rich for the sake of contrast.' I paused. Though you were now watching me with some interest, it was as if from far off and through a mist of reflections concerning persons and subjects unknown.

'Come,' I said urgently. 'You are tired. The wind is cold. Let us step into the Casa Stefano on the corner and have a cup of coffee.'

You laughed. The sight of your uneven teeth between your lips at the bottom of your pinched and ghostly face sent such a wonderful shiver down me that I hardly knew what I was saying any more. I could have flung myself upon you, there and then, and eaten you.

'What a marvellous smile you have,' I muttered feverishly in your ear. 'The Casa Stefano is not much frequented at this hour. Also they have the wireless on permanently. We shall be able to talk quite privately and freely. I mean, if the things that make you laugh are rather unusual, you needn't be afraid of their being overheard.'

'No, no, I'm not afraid,' you protested faintly.

'Of course you aren't,' I instantly rejoined. 'What is there to alarm the most retiring mouse in my proposal? May I take your arm?' This was in order to get you safely into the café before you stopped dead and tried to say good-bye. I had a definite feeling that you contemplated such action. It was impossible to be sure, however, particularly if one took into account your next observation, which was: 'I wasn't thinking of having a Turkish bath.'

'Oh, you can't imagine how glad I am to hear that,' I murmured in an ecstasy. 'Your lovely whiteness steamed into an awful dripping scarlet. I couldn't bear it. Not that it's my business to dictate the colour of your skin, or anything else of a personal nature for that matter. Please don't get wrong impressions. I hope I don't give you the idea that I intend liberties of a disagreeable sort. That would distress me very much. All my remarks are meant as utter compliments.'

I held open the door of the Casa Stefano, which was somewhat cluttered with notices saying: *Luncheon Vouchers Accepted; Hot Meals at All Hours; Customers Are Respectfully Requested Not to Bring Their Own Food; Sandwiches To Take Away.* It was rather dark and warm inside. Stefano and his wife were engrossed in conversation with a compatriot who leaned comfortably against the counter and made sudden, surprising, gestures in the air with both hands. The wireless sang and drummed sufficiently.

You glided in front of me, straight to an obscure seat in a corner. I felt myself drawn along behind, as if by magnetic force. I was certain that I had reached the end of my quest. This time I had found what I needed. My wrists trembled as I carried the coffee to the table.

'You have a ready tongue,' you remarked in a composed and distant voice, folding your legs one over the other and fixing me with rather a disconcerting stare. Were those strange green eyes full of secrets, or did they merely denote unbalance? Both possibilities fascinated me.

'But your name, your name,' I whispered in a kind of screech. 'Our acquaintance is so short that we have not even introduced ourselves properly. Yet I feel as though I'd known you a long time. No. As if I'd known you a long time *ago* and we were meeting again.'

'Nancy Strumbold,' you stated flatly, sipping the coffee in an abstracted way that showed you didn't taste it.

'Strumbold!' I exclaimed. 'Nancy! How individual. How marvellous. I'm a student of names, among other things. I believe far more can be gleaned from them than people realize. It's a neglected science, or art, whichever you prefer to call it. I once wrote a very interesting article on the subject, drawing unusual comparisons of different sorts, touching on alliterative nomenclature amongst our Anglo-Saxon ancestors and ending with a short application of my principles to some famous families of today. It was a great creative and, indeed, analytic effort and I was proud of it. Unfortunately, it clashed with a tidal wave along the south coast by which many people were swept away and drowned, some in the evening of their days, and others mere hopeful kids. At first, my editor thought that if he cut the end off, it would fit at the bottom of the page. But, more news of bodies being washed up and found stuck in trees coming in, it was crowded out altogether. Do you smoke?'

'Yes. What's your name, then?'

As the match flamed between us, your nose seemed immensely long, your dead-white face traversed by extraordinary lines and undulations, your eyes huge. 'Joseph Platt,' I muttered incoherently. 'We must smoke together frequently. I believe it to be conducive to harmonious relationships, as well as soothing to the nerves in a general sense. Sir Walter Raleigh was, I think, one of the first Englishmen to discover the virtues of tobacco — why consider the claims of foreigners? I'm against it, at any rate. Sir Walter found regular smoke greatly alleviated the tedium of incarceration in the Tower of London. One doesn't have to be shut up in a fortress to appreciate his feelings. One has had sensations of imprisonment often enough. Oh, my God! No, what I mean is ... is....' I struggled for words, a problem I did not often have to solve. Seldom did I falter, once my mouth was open.

'Did you say Platt?' you remarked, as if nothing whatever had happened. 'I'm sure I never heard the name before. We can't have met as you thought. It must have been somebody else.'

'All the better,' I said faintly. 'It means a new beginning. What has previous history to do with situations such as ours? Two wanderers met in the street. Two shades murmuring under cover of a wireless.' I gazed at the empty chairs and tables which stretched between us and the three Italians at the counter. They had a bright light there that shone down on them directly and made the shadows of their gestures slide sharply, boldly over the floor and across some of the tables nearest to them. They held their heads close together and their hands were seldom still.

You yawned politely behind your fingers.

4

WHEN he had written this much, Joseph was overcome by exhaustion and lay supine on the sofa, his mind incapable, his face quite pale, the pen and paper on the floor. In a minute, he thought drowsily, I'll have a drop of whiskey, a cigarette, a biscuit. I believe the time has come to celebrate, to drink your health and mine. For I feel I have at last got properly started on my masterpiece; this shrine I am endeavouring to erect to your precious memory. If only writing were not such damnable hard work, he sighed, lying even flatter on the cushions and fixing a vacant gaze on the cupboard full of notebooks. He wondered how he had ever had the energy, or persistence, to cover so many sheets of paper with descriptions of the same subject. I just never get tired of it, he murmured voluptuously.

Waking from a short sleep, he sprang instantaneously to his feet in great anxiety. Was it true, as he had dreamed, that all those pages he had just written, at such cost to his strength and general constitution, were filled with lies? Are nothing but a travesty of you, darling, and the wonderful things you said in the Casa Stefano? I see you so clearly in imagination, enthroned in your corner, the most extraordinary pronouncements whistling though your teeth. For it can't be denied that you had a curiously sibilant enunciation and were inclined to spit. But perhaps it was not noticeable on that first occasion. It grew on you distinctly as years went by. You may also have restrained

14

yourself, being aware of the habit, as I discovered afterwards. Not that I'd have objected. You know that perfectly. On the contrary, it had an inexpressible attraction. You remember how I used to like you to sit with your profile against the light when we were talking.

Why am I so abominably confused? he muttered, reading swiftly through his manuscript, the greatest agitation throbbing in his head and making it quite difficult to focus on the sense. It is as I feared: your epochal contributions have been entirely omitted. There's only me, me, me all down the page. Very likely, I never said any of these things at that time, but thought of them later, or on different occasions, or took them from books, speeches, newspapers and television titbits.

Yet, on going through it again, more calmly, it struck him as having a foundation of truth. He was pretty sure he had expressed most of the sentiments recorded. It was our first meeting and you were naturally shy and what with that and my wish to put you at your ease, chiefly by avoiding awkward silences, I may have become more loquacious than I realized. No, the chief fault is that it's much too short. We remained in the Casa Stefano for hours, occasionally buying new cups of coffee in order to pacify Stefano, his wife and friend, who were certainly planning some grand conspiracy and might otherwise have suspected us of being spies.

I remember you were afraid of that, having recently seen a film very reminiscent of our present situation. Even though I explained, fully and with a wealth of vivid detail, the workings of the Mafia and demonstrated incontestably that they did not function in this country, you were not reassured. On the contrary, for reasons not altogether clear to me even now, my vehemence and the professional delight I took in composing lively descriptions seemed to alarm you further. The more I said, the greater was your conviction that Stefano was planning our destruction. His features recalled an illustration to a story you had read not long ago.

'I made a careful note of it a few days later,' he cried, jumping from the sofa in tremendous agitation. 'I know I did. And then, there was my diary too. I'm sure I wrote a dozen separate accounts. Not that the essentials varied—how could they? It was the emotion which fluctuated, causing different lights to fall on my narrative and changing the sense, though not the events, out of all recognition. Sometimes I laid emphasis on your ghostly appearance, hovering in the shadows of that café. Sometimes on those eyes that seemed to speak of countries full of dreams where we might meet more comfortably than on this earth. Again, I might be principally taken with your voice, its harsh nasal intonations ringing in my ears with an extraordinary persistence as I wrote. Oh, Nancy, above everything I used to think at the beginning of our acquaintance: With nothing on, she must be rather hairy.'

As he muttered through these memories, he searched the cupboard, taking down exercise books, pads and bundles of loose sheets, some tied together in places, others not. For a long time he had been occupied with the later stages of his story. It was essential to get the preliminary notes for that straight; to decide on the climax; to elaborate in the right places in order to bring out the truth; to show it in a blinding light, so that no one could ever gainsay it. That is my sole object, darling, he gasped, feeling at the back of the top shelf and bringing out a small piece of paper on which was written: I never said any such thing. Nor did Grandma.

His hand trembled as he stared at this message in an ecstasy. Your own writing, sweetheart. How did it get

16

there? Those wonderfully uneducated loops and twirls. I can see you now, gripping the pen as though it might run off on its own account and talk in a way you would not permit, if it could be prevented. But I mustn't digress. That belongs to another chapter where we were on a slightly changed footing from the period which occupies us now. He flattened the message and placed it tenderly on the mantelpiece, under one of the legs of the clock.

He was searching mainly for a red exercise book with multiplication tables printed on the back; and for eight pads called Acropolis and bearing a small embossed representation of that famous temple on the front. He remembered, most distinctly, buying them in the closing-down sale of a dingy shop of which the proprietor had unexpectedly gone mad; though many people afterwards said he'd been queer for a long period and it didn't surprise them in the least when he was discovered on the roof, threatening to fling himself on to the pavement because certain unnamed officials, who had no right to do so, were pursuing him with false accusations of a particularly disgusting kind. 'Poor man,' sighed Joseph sympathetically. What he must have gone through.

There was no sign of the Acropolis on the second shelf. He could have sworn he'd seen them quite recently, piled in the right- or left-hand corner. Certainly one or the other. Why, he could even recall that the red book had been on top of the eight pads and had reflected a rosy glow on the underneath of the shelf above. He had, altogether, four red books, dealing with subsequent episodes in his projected history. He had bought them at the same time as the Acropolis pads. The covers had had a particular smell he found difficult to describe.

He reached himself another drink and started on the next shelf, quickly taking handfuls of paper, flicking through them in an instant and placing them on the floor. The rain murmured an incessant background to his work. He could hear high heels clicking sharply on the pavement beneath the unending procession of umbrellas, some moving north and the rest south.

It was amazing how many people found it necessary to be out on a day like this. Perhaps they had not enough food in the house to last them through the night, he thought, leaning dreamily on his table for a breather, chin on fists. Or surprising news might have spread in the town, causing this unusual restlessness. If it was unusual. His preoccupations were generally so intense that he scarcely noticed what went on outside his window. It might be that they always promenaded at this hour, for domestic or other reasons not fully explained, and he had never chanced to pause and notice them.

'But it's essential to waste no more time,' he muttered urgently. 'Those pads are somewhere. It's a good while since I wrote, or read, them, yet the opening words of each are quite familiar to me. They concerned you, darling, and your state of mind and what we said and how your grandma reacted. Why, I could quote whole paragraphs if I tried.'

Instead of trying, he began snatching things off the remaining shelves as though his life depended on it. What had been neat piles on the hearthrug became untidy heaps, collapsed and spilling into an anonymous mass of old, yellowed paper, faintly incised with pencil, ink, crayon, whatever he had happened to grasp when seized by the overwhelming need to write. But now he was coming down to new books, filled only last year, or the year before. It was possible, of course, that the red exercise book and eight pads had got out of place and been mixed up with this much more recent stuff.

18

The pads he was looking for were definitely of a greyish colour. Or, they might seem to have rather a blue tinge, especially in artificial light. Or, was it only that the name and trade device were stamped in blue? 'But why do I puzzle my brains with such questions?' he cried in despair. 'I must keep my attention on what I'm doing, in case of missing important clues. And it's bad for me to get overwrought. I feel giddy. I feel I shall never find them, darling, nor any of the treasures they contain.'

He sank back on his heels, breathless with worry. The passing footsteps sounded extraordinarily loud. Could there be a protest meeting somewhere? If so, he had an inclination to rush out of the house and join it. 'I'd vote for all the resolutions,' he whispered. 'The more and the worse they were, the better. I'd cast two votes, one for each of us. Because, though I have a horror of organizations and have never belonged to any, yet I think protests and resolutions most important. If only one had time for everything and a more reliable memory. Can I have left them in one of the cupboards downstairs, upstairs, in the box-room?'

It seemed that he would have to examine the unused parts of the house. Much time had passed since he had done more than hastily put his head round the doors and take it back again. He ought never to have succumbed to those fears. No, that was too strong a word. 'Distaste' was better. The unaccountable shrinkings of an artist which were the essence, or very near it, of his gifts. All such people were strange. How could it be declared a normal thing for a man to be so madly enamoured of words, their rhythms, sounds and meanings, that he devoted his life to arranging and rearranging them in different patterns?

'It's perfectly reasonable for a man like me to be nervous,' he thought, treading firmly down the stairs. There would be something wrong with me if I wasn't. It would show that my sensitivities had been blunted and my poetic awareness of the emanations of the past begun to decline. Now that would really give cause for alarm and upset. Your whole reputation, and mine too, depends on my keeping going a long while yet. Right to the end, darling, whatever that may be.

Though he pursued these ruminations with vigour, he did not feel particularly reassured. The idea of searching those rooms remained dreadful. 'I'm a fool,' he cried, impatiently flinging open the nearest door. 'Anyone would think the place was full of ghosts, or poisonous gases of some sort. Fiddlesticks.'

The curtains were drawn, but a good deal of light percolated through and round them, because age had reduced them to shreds. A large grey mound in the centre of the floor indicated the last resting place of the furniture. One could see legs, feet, fringes, folds, protruding here and there. 'I believe she had a candelabra, too,' he murmured, stepping past on tiptoe. He searched for footprints near the window and could see none. The dust was thick and even over the marks of his last visit. Afraid to pull back the curtains this time, in case they disintegrated in his hand, he very gingerly hitched the ends round an adjacent flower pot containing slight traces of a dead plant.

But he must not continue to delay. It was absolutely necessary to open the cupboard, no matter what happened. 'As if anything unexpected could occur,' he muttered incoherently, seizing the knob and pulling sharply. 'I know what I shall see. I don't even have to look. One would think the shelves were packed with corpses or, at best, the most dreadful secrets, the way I'm going on.' When he actually saw the papers tumbling out, he turned pale. A cloud of dust rose up, as from an explosion, as they hit the ground and slid to every corner. He could have sworn there had not been half so many on his last inspection.

How was it possible to check through these in quest of those he sought? Innumerable, unindexed, indecipherable, they lay in pale oblongs, squares and fans and stars between him and the door. Dust was already beginning to settle on them. 'The most essential, the most important, fact to remember,' he chattered, 'is that time has strict limits. I literally can't afford to stop and sort them. Also, now that I come to think of it, I never had the red book, or the Acropolis series in here at all. I'm certain of that.'

He was trembling and shivering to an extraordinary degree, but that may have been due to the damp; and the close atmosphere; and the exhaustion of overwork; and the fact that one of old Mrs Strumbold's gloves had unaccountably lodged itself between the bars of the empty grate. How had he never noticed it before? It was one of her best gloves. He remembered it plainly. She used to wear them on her Sunday outings.

He rushed from the place. In the hall he felt easier and paused. All the unoccupied rooms were full of dust and sheeted furniture. Each one had cupboards crammed with papers of every size and content. Who knew what the writings said, or meant? Whether he was the author of the whole or only part? Whether a percentage were not blank sheets, spare books, ready for his busy pen but never employed? He had long been addled on this point and quite unable to give a clear answer to such questions.

For some minutes he stood at the bottom of the stairs considering. One oughtn't to decide important matters in a hurry. Extra time should be allowed for exhaustion, confusion and any degree of nervous debility from which one might happen to suffer. People differed in their resilience to these things. Some might have gone straight on with the task, not stopping until the last drawer had been emptied, the last shelf examined. Others would require an interval of repose, though not necessarily of a weak constitution. No. The explanation, in their case, was a greater percipience and sensitivity to atmosphere. They simply could not endure it, for reasons unconnected with physique, monotonous diet and lack of fresh air. These were shy dreamers, needing hours and days before they could screw themselves up to such definite action as ransacking a house where all the rooms were full of contradictory whisperings and sudden mementoes, such as half a pair of Sunday gloves unaccountably inserted between the bars of a grate, as if wishing to be incinerated.

'Yet, darling,' he muttered, sinking down on the lowest step, 'my whole happiness is contained within these walls. You are here. I feel you as I open the gate and again, very strongly, as the door swings slowly under my hand. When I'm away, wherever I am, whatever adulations are being addressed to me, I remember this marvellous oasis constantly, this patch of wild jungle that is our home. It gives me an aloofness and a strangeness that people find impressive and take for a sign of genius, if admirers; of madness, or arrogance, if not.

'I mustn't allow myself to wander,' he cried, tears rolling down his face. 'Am I, or am I not, to persevere in the search after those essential materials for my next chapter? I can, of course, manage without them to a certain extent, but my account will then lack that superlative degree of verisimilitude at which I aim. For they were notes made at the time. I'm pretty sure of that. They record your actual words and observations, your conclusions, sweetheart, arrived at after a review of all relevant facts.'

Even as these thoughts ran through his mind, he wondered whether it was truly so. The doubt distressed him greatly, not only of itself but also because it put off the solution of his problems almost to infinity. 'I can't let that happen,' he said with attempted firmness, squeezing his fingers together. 'It's essential to be practical in a crisis. How hungry I am, for instance. Maybe food's the answer. I believe a plate of bacon and eggs would enable me to get to the root of it.' He laughed happily at this new idea, his depression sliding back into the dark place from which it had come. 'I'll do it, never fear!' he shouted in a voice that fled from wall to wall and up and down the stairs until it died away into a mutter, stifled by the silence waiting everywhere.

Now that he had definitely decided not to continue the search — at least, not for the moment — quietness was once more his friend. Next week, or the week after, on a day when the rooms were full of sunshine, he would look through a few boxes and cupboards first thing in the morning, before he got tired. The mistake had been to embark on such a very taxing labour after a severe stint of writing when his nerves were frayed. One needed to be in perfect trim, physically and mentally. That was why he visited the empty parts of the house so seldom. He hardly ever felt equal to it. One required to be washed in through the doors on a wave of euphoria.

His meditation was interrupted by sharp knocking and ringing. He reached out and turned the handle. There, in the porch, against the misty background of perpetual rain, stood a small dark person, his lips curved sweetly into a smile, his hair stuck to his head, his shoes sodden. Leaning an umbrella on the wall, the man said: 'May I speak to the lady of the house?'

'That's quite impossible,' Joseph replied, staring at the apparition intently.

'I wouldn't detain her long. I believe she would be very

interested,' the other persisted, giving a perfunctory smirk.

'The lady left a long while ago,' said Joseph vaguely. 'I'm alone.'

'Oh, I'm sorry to hear that, sir,' said the man, with a look of false sympathy. 'In that case, I think I can interest *you* particularly.' He flicked open a little suitcase he had. 'Qwikcleen Mop and Brush Co. Our mops and brushes are specially designed for the busy housewife. No corner is too small for them. No area too large. One wipe, one brush, and your work's done. Instant cleanliness with Qwikcleen. Each brush and mop is evenly impregnated with Qwikcleen Magic Grease Remover. No more smeary plates. No more patchy floors, paintwork, tiles, carpets, cookers, baths, basins, toilets.'

Rattling off his piece with amazing velocity, he spread brushes and mops of every shape and pastel colouring all over the porch. Some leaned on the wall; some lay on the step; some stood in the suitcase; or curved round its edge — these were for difficult corners; or peeped coyly out of plastic bags — these were mainly pink and intended for mopping and brushing babies with the minimum of inconvenience. They were universally small and of a slippery material, Joseph noted, evidently designed for quick-fingered midgets.

Rain dripped on to them from the salesman as he stooped over his task, murmuring: 'Qwikcleen for every household task. Enter the Qwikcleen Competition and win a dream house, fully fitted and ready to walk into. Instructions with every container of Qwikcleen Emulsion Cleanser.'

How you would have adored this, darling, Joseph thought. How you would have been gulled by this sad midget crook, with his mops and brushes populating the doorstep like a miniature audience staring up as you stood, an outsize giant on a stage in front of them.

Hearing no reaction to his chatter, the salesman paused and looked into Joseph's absent face. Nuts! was his immediate conclusion, based on the experience of innumerable doorsteps, in every kind of neighbourhood, even the most unpromising. For one couldn't neglect the smallest opening in his trade. He had no personal objection to madmen. Sometimes they were quite free with their money. He had once sold a lunatic seventeen lavatory brushes. But his trader's instinct warned him that this one would merely shut the door in the end, without so much as a thank you, or good day.

As he glanced round the garden and into the hall, certain stories he had heard during previous expeditions began to come back to him. He was accustomed to gossip in public houses during the evenings, often getting useful tips and background information thus. There were three bars in the vicinity and in all he had heard the same sort of thing, rather more obscene in the 'George', as his informant was especially drunk; more circumstantial in the 'Anchor', where it was not so near closing time and they still had a hold on their wits; altogether incredible at the 'Duke'. He stepped back into the rain and looked up at the name board over the porch. As he had thought, it said: The Nook.

Joseph leaned slackly on the doorpost, hands in pockets, while his visitor gathered up his multi-coloured wares and stuffed them into the case. He did not seem surprised at the sudden departure. One could not be sure that he had noticed it. His eyes were full of excitement, plans, projects, memories, vistas of extraordinary import.

5

I SHALL always remember, darling, the day I first visited your home, Joseph wrote industriously. We had had several more sessions in the Casa Stefano by that time. You generally expressed a certain reluctance to enter, but I insisted, convinced that it was only shyness; what else could it signify?

'I know what it is to be shy myself,' I said reassuringly. 'I've struggled with it for years. Ah, you can't imagine the desperate trials I've undergone, half faint with terror before an appointment, blushing with fright at the sound of my own voice. You wouldn't think it now, would you?'

'No,' you said, hesitating in midstep as if you meditated a sudden flight sideways.

'I only tell you these things to encourage you,' I continued, firmly grasping your arm. 'Many persons afterwards famous have suffered similarly. But it's more homely and more intimate,' I said, with the faintest squeeze of your elbow, 'to draw one's examples from that stratum of humanity with which one is familiar. Why, if I had ever met a prince in flesh and blood, I'd use him to illustrate my meaning. The nearest I got to royalty was a certain black man who swore his father was a king. If I would lend him a hundred pounds, he said, and allow him to use my name on HP forms and when negotiating with landladies; not only would he offer fifty per cent interest and repayment within six months, but he would take me on a visit to his country.'

'I hate bad smells,' you said.

'So do I!' I cried. 'My very first question to this pseudo prince concerned the sanitation in his native land. He said his royal father had installed a full-flush system in the palace. The fittings were on the small side, having been made by Japs for Japs and bought second-hand from an Arab. He assured me that they were perfectly adequate, for all that. During the rainy season, when the cisterns were full, one could hear nothing but flush, flush, flush, as one approached the palace. Some of the lesser queens were rather young and had been bought in out-of-the-way places where such refinements, though talked of, had never actually been seen, much less operated.'

'How funny,' you remarked, more relaxed now that we had passed the Casa Stefano.

The days were always fine then, darling, as I remember; the sun shone warmly at the upper floors of the buildings. We could see it glittering on the windows and it was possible to imagine the people up there working in their shirt-sleeves. Some of the roofs had flagpoles on them and we could just distinguish the various colours against the intense blue of the sky. We stood at the bus stop, gazing into the air and counting.

When your number came and I boarded it also, you seemed discomposed, protesting, 'You've never done this before. Where are you going?'

'Nancy,' I said earnestly, though in a subdued voice, so that the passengers before and behind should not overhear too clearly, 'I must come with you. It is destiny. I feel it strongly. Don't be alarmed. How easily upset you are by the smallest unexpected thing. You turn so wonderfully white. Forgive me if my attentions are a little pressing sometimes. I can't help it. Yet what have I ever done except squeeze your hand and hold your arm and talk, rivers and cataracts of talk to put you at your ease and save you the trouble of trying to be interesting?'

'I don't know,' you said.

'Well, then,' I rejoined triumphantly, 'what of it? Why should we complain, since we are both suited by a situation which might not agree with everyone, but fits us to a T? Many persons wealthier than we are, and also higher up the social scale, have searched for our contentment unavailingly. I know this from my labours as a gossip columnist. It was my business to winkle out secrets. Or, where there weren't any, to write in a manner suggesting, even to the most inattentive reader, whole worlds and underworlds kept locked and barred in perpetuity.'

Thus we journeyed, darling, bouncing together on the hard seat. Your home was at the terminus. It would have been more comfortable and quicker to go by train, but the ticket was twice as much, you explained; and the station a great deal farther from The Nook than the bus stop.

'The Nook,' I repeated happily. 'That's a delightful name. Why didn't you tell me of it long ago? I've lived in The Laurels, The Willows, The Elms and The Firs—at one time I'd a passion for trees—but never The Nook. It seems so right for someone like you. I can imagine you peeping out of the windows first thing in the morning and locking the doors before going to bed.'

A very vivid picture rose in my mind of your pale skinny legs racing up a dark flight of stairs as if pursued by the sound of your own footsteps, rat-tat-tat on the bare boards. 'Aha,' I sighed lingeringly. 'It's not a block of flats, by any chance, is it?'

'Oh, no,' you said, screwing your gloves which showed signs of a severe course of such treatment, 'Grandma and I have the place to ourselves.'

I took the gloves and smoothed them on my knee as well as I could for the bus was lurching madly. As I stroked, I said in what I hoped was a truly reassuring voice: 'I guessed you had a grandma, though you didn't say so. Do you believe in telepathy? I've come across many remarkable instances during my peregrinations in search of unusual news and views. And not only between close relatives where you might expect it, such as identical twins, for instance. Actually, I have always refused to have to do with identical twins because there is something about them that gives me the horrors.'

'I think it would be rather fun — to be one, I mean,' you said.

I twisted round to look at you properly, thinking: what if she were two, both so alike I couldn't tell which I was embracing? Since the horrible thing about them is that they give the impression of being only half a person each, it would be necessary to have both to get any satisfaction at all. That I believe to be the root of my aversion. I wouldn't be able to manage it and my fear that I am unusually feeble in such situations would be fully realized. It may be that I love my darling Nancy so much just for the reason that she is not altogether keen on sex and will always make me feel a great, big, insatiable brute.

My whole body glowed with joy as this thought swam round and round my head. We were jolting along a suburban road and you were gazing at the flowering trees growing in the pavement and spreading a pink mist in front of the houses, which all had tall, twisted chimneys, bow windows and large knockers on the doors. The sun was able to reach ground level here, to nourish the daffodils, hyacinths and early tulips we saw through the garden fences.

I snuggled up to you, murmuring urgently, 'Is it much further? Is it a house like these? What age is your grandma?'

'Eighty-eight,' you replied in a low voice.

'Oh, Nancy,' I cried, shivering and trembling from head to foot, 'what an exciting person you are! Every time we meet, you come out with something new and strange. It's an education to be in your company. I speak as a man of the world. Eighty-eight, you said? I've never met anyone so ancient, though I was once engaged to go round old folk's homes and write a piece explaining how they had preserved themselves so long. But I could come on nobody over eighty-six, though several centenarians were supposed to be living in the district. Perhaps they were too daft to be presentable. Not that I should have minded. The keepers did me an injustice there.'

'What did they say had kept them alive?' you asked in peculiarly flat tones.

'Why, some said it was due to plenty of drink and smoke. Others put it down to having taken the pledge as young persons, under the influence of attractive parsons. Or, they had always walked instead of riding in buses. Or done exercises at open windows every morning. Or cold baths. Or no baths, no exercise to wear away the tissues, no dieting, nothing smacking of exertion.'

You listened attentively to this rigmarole and, as I paused for breath, put in: 'Grandma's rather stagnant.'

'I'm looking forward so much to meeting her,' I cried. 'I can't tell you ... stagnant or not ... eighty-eight.... The whole idea thrills me. I couldn't afford to continue the researches into old age I was speaking of just now. My editor didn't take up the subject with sufficient enthusiasm, especially as an aeroplane accident happened almost at once. Everyone was killed, many of them honeymoon couples. Handbags, photos and other affecting mementoes were strewn widely over the mountainside beneath which the happy shouts of, "Good-bye! Enjoy yourselves!" had scarcely died away before tragedy struck. But here, surely, is the terminus. Wake up, Nancy. It is the bus station. Everyone is getting off. We have reached the end of our journey in perfect safety.'

So saying, I got up and dragged you after me. 'Which way now?' I demanded as we stepped on to the road. 'All directions look the same in neighbourhoods like these. But that's only a deceptive appearance they have. Whole volumes and series could be written on this theme, with pretentious general titles, such as, The Rhythm of Time, or The Music of the Sphere; and snappy little tags for individual instalments like, Squares and Circles, or, Ripples. I declare I shall do it myself, one day, simply to prove I'm not the negligible quantity people have often thought. Have you ever considered, Nancy, why writers write?'

'No,' you said. 'Why are we walking so fast?'

'Because it's impossible to proceed at a snail's pace on an occasion like the present,' I answered vehemently. 'On a spring day. On the way to a momentous meeting with an old person of eighty-eight. For I feel quite sure that this bus ride, culminating in my first sight of The Nook, partakes of destiny. Nothing will ever be the same again, I assure you. Have you no sensations of a similar kind?'

'How you do gabble,' you said.

'Of course I do!' I cried with the greatest animation I was capable of, considering that the speed at which we were travelling left small reserves of breath. 'Only by gabble-gobble-gabble can one hope to bridge the awful gulfs surrounding one on every side. The howling wilderness. I was once given a free ticket to a play on the subject. It made a tremendous impression on me, partly because I so seldom attended the drama, for lack of funds. Your grandma isn't daft, by any chance, is she?'

'No,' you said, with some asperity.

'Don't take me up wrongly,' I chattered, full of an all but inexplicable happiness. 'As I said before, with reference to my experiences among old folks, daftness doesn't in the least upset me. On the contrary, I find it full of a subtle charm. In a way, it inspires me more than anything. If only there hadn't been that honeymoon aeroplane crash, I might have written some striking stuff. I might now be looked up to, sought after, instead of as you see. What, is this the place?'

You had suddenly stopped and put your hand on a gate. Looking up, I saw The Nook painted over the porch. An extraordinary sensation of peace and well-being suffused me, as if I had found a prize after many false clues followed to the bitter end; or had at last succeeded in a long and difficult task. Instead of leading the way with large gesticulations, as was my habit, I fell in behind you like a somnambulist. Thus, we glided up the path close together and you put your key in the lock.

6

'AND that was how I began my imprisonment in this place,' cried Joseph, flinging his pen down on the table so that it skidded over to the window-sill. 'That was the way I was enticed into my servitude. I shall never be free. I know it now. Not even though I were dragged out by force and the house smashed to bits with a battering ram and a block of luxury maisonettes with fitted kitchens, central heating and garages substituted.

'What am I saying? I don't mean that at all. No, no. On the contrary. Those days were paradisal. I experienced nothing like them on this earth before, or since. How can I recapture what I felt as you pushed the door and over your shoulder I smelt the mixture of floor polish, frying and cheaply scented soaps which permeated every room? As I observed the brown linoleum, the dark paint, the semi-twilight caused by net curtains, potted plants and too much furniture?'

Standing idly in the middle of his piled manuscripts, Joseph inhaled again those old, stale airs. Mrs Strumbold did not care to have the windows opened and most of them had been fast stuck for years. Sometimes the rooms were hot and breathless; sometimes pervaded by a peculiarly penetrating cold stuffiness. It depended mainly on the time of year. No wonder you always looked so pale, darling, he thought. Yet, perhaps you, too, might have lived to ninety-one, had circumstances permitted. There can't have been anything really unhealthy in the atmosphere. We all flourished in our different ways. Especially me.

A warm glow spread over his whole body and he began feeling for his pen amongst the cluttered papers on the table. 'Why, one is always a prisoner to something,' he murmured. 'What would I be without my chains? A miserable little journalist in a miserable little rag. My long incarceration has saved me. I believe if all my doors and windows were suddenly flung open, I'd never rest until I got them shut again.' He pictured himself running frantically from point to point and stopping up the apertures. It would be a terrible experience, like plugging leaks in the aquarium in which one swam before the precious water disappeared. The level would get lower and lower, the liquid thicker, one's energy correspondingly decline. Would one have the strength, the organization and the skill to complete the task before being suffocated in unaccustomed air? That was the exciting question.

Shall I last till eighty-eight, or ninety-one? he wondered. Shall I be cut down in my prime? He leaned his face on the window pane and stared through it with a strange fixed smile. The rain was not quite so much today. There was even a suspicion of watery sun at times. The people passing up and down were more animated. They stepped out with some confidence and addressed occasional remarks to each other, though Joseph could not hear what they said. One or two pointed up at him. But perhaps they did not really see him and intended to indicate something on the roof; or a rare kind of aeroplane flying above. It may be that I'm invisible to them, he thought, sinking luxuriously into the hollows of his sofa, pen in hand.

We pushed into the hall at once, darling; this very hall I've cherished ever since and kept exactly as it was on that first day, as far as I've been able. There's less soap, less

34

frying and more dust. Apart from that, I don't believe you'd notice any difference, were it possible for you to come back on a tour of inspection.

A sharp old voice cried, 'Nancy, have you remembered the butter? I see you've brought your boyfriend to visit me at last, and the supper will be spartan if you've forgotten the butter.'

A small twisted person appeared at the end of the passage. She had a very individual hobbling gait that got her over the ground with amazing celerity. In a second, she was close under my chin and squinting up into my face. 'You're Joseph, I suppose?'

'Madam,' I said, detaching a gnarled hand from my coat and bending low over it, 'I have long looked forward to the privilege of meeting a person so eminent in years as yourself. I say this in all sincerity and for special reasons which Nancy can enumerate, if you wish, because I explained the whole matter to her on the bus. We have brought butter, bread and haddock.'

'You didn't tell me he was an actor, Nancy,' Mrs Strumbold remarked. 'How secretive you are.' She swivelled round so as to view me in a better light and I could see the white hairs on her chin trembling. 'She never tells me anything if she can help it,' the old woman continued in a confidential voice. 'Either I have to surprise it out of her, or else put two and two together.'

'But that is one of the most charming things about her,' I rejoined, staring down eagerly into those boot-button-eyes.

'Oh, is it,' said Mrs Strumbold.

Meanwhile, you were taking the provisions out of the small case in which you carried sandwiches, novels, sweets, cosmetics and other comforts to help bring you safely through the day. I wondered why you had tried by every means to avoid introducing me to your home, even calling your grandma 'stagnant', an unsuitable epithet to apply to the person now before me. You might have guessed that I would find her perfectly delightful. As I watched you, Mrs Strumbold examined me with the careful attention one bestows on a moderately priced suit of clothes hanging in a shop; or on a cheap joint of meat one hopes will prove both succulent and tender. A bar of sunlight, coming through the open door, illumined the three of us in the narrow hall.

I began to chatter: 'The haddock's rather meagre, I'm afraid, because it wasn't decided until the last moment that I should come with Nancy. Though I have waited many months for the honour of making your acquaintance, Mrs Strumbold, only at the actual bus stop, after all possible shopping had been done, was the invitation extended to me.'

'Stuff,' said Mrs Strumbold in a surprised voice.

'On the contrary, madam,' I said warmly, 'every word I speak is, as it were, on oath. Nothing is more abhorrent to me than specious compliments, arguments, and empty talk in general. But to get back to the safe neutrality of haddock: there was no convenient fishmonger where we could have supplemented our previous purchase. I should like you to know that I chose this particular fish and that Nancy was happy to follow my advice; and it is my intention now to cook you the dish with which I won a prize in a margarine competition.'

'Go on,' said Mrs Strumbold, sidling after me into the kitchen.

'Yes,' I insisted. 'It was for the cheapest, tastiest, ten-minute supper, the only condition being that Fulvite margarine must be an important ingredient. Actually, it's much nicer with butter. The prize was a day trip to

36

Boulogne for two. Oh, if I'd known you then, Nancy,' I cried, seizing you suddenly up against the wall and giving you such a kiss and such a squeeze as left you quite confused.

'That's a prize boyfriend you've got there,' Mrs Strumbold remarked to her granddaughter. She sat down at the table. As you began laying a third place, the knife and fork slid out of your hand and crashed on to a plate. Though nothing was broken, you gave a little sob of fright.

'I await your verdict on my culinary efforts, madam,' I immediately said, to distract that formidable old woman's attention and leave you time to recover. 'If, as I devoutly hope, it's favourable, I shall take the liberty of inviting myself again and trying you with another dish from my repertoire.'

You knocked over a glass and Grandma smacked her lips. I was now in my shirtsleeves and with one of your aprons tied round me. 'Yes, madam,' I continued, greatly encouraged, 'I at one time took up the study of low-cost nutrition quite seriously. I was broke, as I don't mind admitting between friends. I could not afford to dine out unless paid for, except in places too low and dirty even for bankrupts like me. So I experimented with the trimmings of meat usually sold for dogs, and the heads and tails of fish as delivered to the addresses of high-class cats. I found — as indeed is often the case in life — that a little ingenuity worked wonders.'

Mrs Strumbold began sniffing appreciatively and said: 'I wonder you never brought this boyfriend here before, Nancy. It's a long while since we had anything decently cooked. When your pleasures have been cut down through old age, you begin to dwell on the ones that are left. I do, I know.' She smiled at me, showing an expanse of false teeth. As Grandma became more genial, you grew correspondingly paler and now sat on a wooden stool with a puzzling air of having been arrested and locked into a police station. I was so much struck by your appearance that I had some difficulty in attending to my saucepan.

'I decided to bring out a book of recipes,' I went on in a distracted voice. 'It was my first published work, apart from my contributions to gossip columns. I called it *Gorging on a Shoestring*. For dogs' pieces and fish heads, I substituted stewing steak, cod, haddock, herrings.'

'This boyfriend is a remarkable actor, Nancy,' said Mrs Strumbold, grasping her knife and fork strongly in her crooked hands. 'I believe he would bring the house down as Hamlet.'

Suddenly you screamed, opening your mouth wide and throwing back your head as far as it would go.

'What's the matter with her?' I cried. But Mrs Strumbold only looked malignant. 'Darling,' I exclaimed, taking your rigid body in my arms. 'You haven't been well all the evening. I sensed it in the fishmonger's, on the bus, and said nothing from a mistaken idea of tact and delicacy. I took it for a woman's ailment. But how wrong I was. You should be in bed. Come, let's go upstairs and I'll bring your supper when you have recovered. What a fortunate coincidence that I should be here on this particular day. I believe I said something to the effect that it was a time of destiny for us. Nancy, Nancy, I can hardly bear the excitement.'

So speaking, I urged you up the dark stairs, the very stairs that I traversed not half an hour ago. You did not resist and gave an impression of utter weariness, of having abandoned a struggle against overwhelming odds.

'But there is no need to worry any more,' I whispered close beside your ear. 'I will see to everything. I have resolved on it for both our sakes.' These words went sliding up the wall ahead of us like a portent. You did not answer, only giving a faint sigh and stumbling slightly at the next step.

'Your bedroom,' I continued in a muted screech, 'which door is it? Your room? Your room? Hush, darling, don't tremble so. There's no need to be alarmed. It is simply that I want to avoid an intrusion on Grandma's private domain. I don't like the idea of seeing her curlers, underclothes and whatever else she has scattered about. She wouldn't care for it, I'm sure. After all, it's the first time she's met me.'

I had managed to subdue my voice into a soothing monotone during the latter part of this speech. Consequently, you were able to indicate the left-hand door. which I opened to reveal a small, low room looking over the back garden. On one wall was a mirror, above a table, and opposite a coloured photograph of a spaniel that seemed, at a hurried glance, to have been part of a calendar. A hard, narrow bed was jammed into the corner behind the door.

'Lie down at once, sweetheart,' I commanded warmly. 'You need rest. Your nerves are overstrained and I don't wonder at it, now that I see the circumstances in which you live with my own eyes. Heavens, what burdens you carry on those wonderfully slender shoulders whose blades fascinate me, even through substantial coats. Not a word, I insist.' You had opened your mouth. 'Let me take off your shoes.'

As I bent tenderly over your foot, you kicked me in the face, shouting, 'Don't touch me! Get out! Go away! Damn you, damn you, damn you!'

I judged it best to leave you to recover on your own. Women were supposed to benefit from a good cry. Even the mildest were subject to tantrums at intervals. My experiences in the newspaper world had taught me that much. I longed to give you one more kiss, but resisted.

Something in your distraught face appealed to me immensely. I shall never forget that moment, darling. Whenever I cross the landing, I'm reminded of it, so vividly at times that I open the door and look at your bed and the mirror, now covered with spots of mould, and the spaniel, faded to a ghost and curled at the edges. I poke my head in just far enough to note these familiar objects. But that's a later chapter.

I stood in the kitchen doorway. Mrs Strumbold was crouched over her plate, demolishing its contents with a peculiar intensity. The shadows collected in her fallen cheeks emphasized the rhythmic power of her jaws. One could imagine her as a cannibal. She made sucking and gasping noises. I stepped softly into the room, saying, 'Does it taste all right?'

'Aha,' she said, the loaded fork halted in front of her nose. 'You startled me. Not that I'm deaf.'

'Preoccupied,' I suggested, sitting down opposite to her and searching that extraordinary face. There were so many incoherent lines and folds about the eyes and round the mouth. On one side she had a twitch. The other was curiously still, as if slightly paralysed. Her glance was like a rodent's: sharp and bright and secretive.

'I started without you,' she remarked, indicating the saucepan. 'Couldn't wait. It smelt so good. You've been damaged, I see.'

'It's nothing,' I said. 'She kicked me. Does she often have these turns?'

'No,' said Mrs Strumbold with the greatest indifference. 'Not so's you'd notice. She gets over it. The doctor did tell me the proper scientific name for it, but I've forgotten. At my age, one can't keep up with science.'

'It's difficult at any age,' I rejoined courteously. 'The ramifications are so vast and specialized. Long and expert study is required before it's safe to open one's mouth on such subjects. Even then, it's only possible to pronounce on some small segment; for instance, the reaction of bats to being kept awake all day.'

'Uhu,' said the old cannibal with marked lack of interest. 'What do you really do for a living?'

'Free-lance,' I said promptly. 'I find it suits my temperament best. The uncertainty stimulates me. The unknown inspires me to greater efforts than I would be capable of under a system of regular hours, graduated superiors and permanent boss.'

'This isn't the first time you've been kicked in the mouth,' she remarked, a shiver of amusement passing over the undulations of her face. 'Have you any money at all?'

'My finances,' I replied with what I hoped sounded like a ready candour, 'go up and down. It is inevitable in a one-man business. There are times when one is worked off one's feet and the cheques pour in. Every stupid idea one has is snapped up at a good price. Those are wonderful days,' I continued dreamily, for it had never yet been my fortune to experience them except in imagination. 'The postman always brings good news. People want to speak to one at parties. They're ready to listen while one explains the higher metaphysics of art. Not that I'm going to at this particular moment. Don't be alarmed. I realize it would be inappropriate. I only mention the matter in order to give you some faint idea of the terrors and rewards of a writer's life.'

'Heh, heh, heh,' laughed the old cannibal, half-choked by the mixture of haddock *au Platt* and a deadly hilarity. 'Heh-heh-wah-wah-heh.' Tears zigzagged down the lines of her cheeks and collected at the point of her jaw. There they sparkled for a moment on the end of a hair before dropping into her plate.

7

IT was in this way that I began my servitude to Grandma Strumbold, Joseph wrote despairingly. No episode in my life has been as humiliating or as fruitful. One of the reasons why I can never forget you, sweetheart, is because you enabled me to know that terrifying phenomenon. Also, you were her flesh and blood.

I began to haunt The Nook. Nothing you said deterred me. I applied myself to the culinary art, inventing new dishes with eggs, mince, macaroni, sausages and other cheap ingredients. I produced soups, cakes, puddings in extraordinary variety. All of these your grandma gobbled up with amazing speed and enjoyment.

'This boyfriend is one in a million,' she would say, wiping round her plate with a bit of bread. 'He was worth waiting for. Her admirers are few and far between,' she'd add to me in a penetrating whisper that I would try to smother with a genteel cough.

For it was never my wish that your feelings should be hurt. Oh, darling, far otherwise. God forbid that I should trample on anybody as vulnerable as you. He took a crumpled photograph from the table and studied it intently. 'How those great big eyes of yours stare up from my hand,' he murmured. 'It's a good likeness of you in certain moods. I took it during one of our walks by the river. We used to walk a lot, as it was the only free amusement to be had.'

He looked out and saw the sun shining through the dripping trees. It was days since he had left the house. Locked in a dreamy struggle with the past, time had evaporated before his pen. Those other seasons had obliterated this. He did not know whether people were really staring up at his window more than they had done of late; or whether he imagined it from an obscure loneliness and desire to be noticed.

I need fresh air and provisions, he thought. There are letters written and waiting to be posted. Even the smallest change of scene would brace me for the next chapter. I believe there's an invitation for this evening, too. He hunted about in the mountain of paper which grew higher every hour, as it seemed, though he knew this could not actually be so. For he had not brought a single sheet from any of the other rooms. He was certain of it. The most he had done was to open a few of the cupboards and try to shut them after a brief inspection. This had not been easy. The mere fact of opening the doors had caused the papers to slide and also to swell in a mysterious way. It had been most difficult and, in some cases actually impossible, to compress them into their former bulk. He did not understand how this could happen, but supposed there must be a scientific explanation. If not, it was a very alarming symptom.

Here was the invitation, at last. He pulled it from the envelope. Yes, as he had thought, it was for tonight at six. He could go out and buy a few things before the shops shut and still catch the five o'clock train. At the party he would be certain to meet admirers. It was days since he had spoken to anyone, much less been flattered, sought after, held an audience captive with his eloquence, his unexpected gestures and general air of finding the world a slightly different place from that observed by his listeners.

He thought of the bright room, the jumbled voices, the drinks, titbits, and cigarettes. As he entered, heads would turn and those who knew him would come forward; and those who had heard of him would watch, rather disappointed at first, for they had expected him to be taller and with a kind of wise severity of countenance he did not possess. Then he would begin talking.

He was quite sure this was the most sensible programme. Much better than remaining a prisoner in a stuffy room. How haggard was his reflection in the mirror. He looked as though he had spent years, rather than days, at his task. The idea occurred to him that perhaps he had been secluded a good deal longer than he thought. Was that why people were staring up at the window more? That was, if they really were. The date on the paper conveyed nothing to him. Nor did the news. It was quite usual for him to have a huge pile of newspapers under his table. He threw them there when he had read them. He examined them only from habit and never remembered any of the items, being supremely indifferent to the aspects of life described and having a strong feeling that everything in them was a lie, or at best, second-hand stuff, cooked up to serve the interests of the moment.

'That shall not be said of our story darling,' he wrote swiftly on a clean page, the invitation still gripped in his left hand. All thoughts of tiredness, hunger, fresh air and recreation vanished as he sank beneath the surface of the only reality he had ever known. Lies have been told, and by me I regret to say, but now at last, in this final redaction, I have reached the truth. It might seem easy just to put down what actually happened; what I witnessed with my own senses and can swear to unhesitatingly. Yet, it is not so. Mountains of paper, ink and painful effort testify to the difficulty of my task, the com-

44

plications, permutations, the endless vigilance required.

It's out of the question to leave the house until I've finished. Food can be ordered over the telephone and delivered. Fresh air may be admitted through the window. Exercise is necessary only to keep-fit fiends. I'm glad to say I've never been that. Oh, Nancy, let us not be separated by another second of extraneous thought. Let us hurry on. Who knows what time is left? Sometimes a desolate feeling comes over me and I doubt. I dare not spare myself. Of what use is it to be rested, to look well, if one's life is perfectly empty? I shall stay here until I am done.

A great sense of happiness and peace swept over him with this declaration. His tiredness lifted. A new face gazed back at him from the mirror. Problems seemed less intractable. For a moment, he even thought he caught sight of her in the looking-glass. 'Oh, that would be wonderful,' he murmured in an ecstasy. 'If you joined me over the mantelpiece. If we lived together again in the glass.' His eyes glittered as he searched the reflected room.

8

I CAME knocking at the gate of The Nook, which had been secured against me in some way, by bars, bolts, wire, or string. 'Hey!' I shouted. 'What's the meaning of this? I come with new recipes for puddings and tarts, with stories designed to amuse the quick and the dead. I guarantee to make time run swiftly and agreeably like a well-oiled train. Why have obstacles been placed in my way? No one's intentions are better than mine. Any disinterested observer will confirm it. Come out at once, Nancy, and undo the gate, or I'll climb it.'

The reason I hesitated to put my threat into execution was the extreme ricketiness of the gate. The wood was rotten everywhere and would collapse as soon as I leant my weight on it. Besides showing me up before the neighbours as a violent character, this would entail subsequent expense and uncongenial work while I repaired it. Circumstances had made me a tolerable handyman, but I got small pleasure from hammering, sawing, screwing, measuring and the hundred other fiddling operations involved in the roughest and most gimcrack carpentry.

So I assaulted the gate in a moderate way, rattling it gingerly, in case of accidents. 'Come out, Nancy,' I called, 'or I shall shout something embarrassing in front of the considerable number of people now listening curiously for my next move. I shall declaim my love on the public footpath, I warn you. My descriptions will be heartfelt and, at the same time, extremely detailed. Let me in! Let me in!'

'It's that boyfriend of yours again,' yelled Grandma from somewhere inside. 'What's up with him? The gate must have stuck. There's been no bolt on it for twenty years, to my certain knowledge. He's got a bee in his bonnet about being shut out. I never met such a boy in my life.'

'Coming, coming,' you panted in a faint voice I could just hear floating through the door. 'Why does he think he's been shut out? He's always got some ridiculous idea in his head. As if it was possible to keep him off.'

'Why try?' returned Mrs Strumbold. 'What other asset have we ever had, I should like to know, since your poor father was drowned off Penang?'

'Don't ask me,' you replied, much dispirited, I thought. 'Sometimes I feel it might have been best if we had all drowned off Penang, or anywhere else for that matter.'

'Stupid girl,' the old woman vociferated with the utmost contempt. 'Fancy wanting a watery grave at your age.'

'Forgive me,' I shouted from the pavement in order to obliterate the worst of Grandma's malice. 'I didn't intend to cause an upset. There's evidently a knack in dealing with this gate. A little instruction is all I need to enable me to arrive at your door like a shadow. To enter the house unannounced,' I whispered, 'as though it were my own. All the rooms and everything in them.'

'What did you say?' You had bent your head right down over the gate in order to deal with the catch. Shadows from the trees moved across your hair like dark hands feeling the shape of your skull.

'I say,' I muttered in an earnest monotone, 'that you oughtn't to distrust me still. Who has laid himself out more to oblige you than I have done? To consider only one facet of my activities, there is the supreme tact I have practised on your grandma. I don't speak of the many

47

meals I have cooked her, because the pleasure I have had from teaching you how to do them more than cancels any trouble I was put to, including the strain on my inventive faculties, which has been severe, I assure you.'

'Yes, yes,' you said at random. 'You have such vitality.'

'Not content with this,' I continued softly, putting my hand over yours, in case you should open before I finished, 'I have mitigated her conduct towards you by putting her in a good frame of mind for hours at a time. There have even been moments when she turned quite gracious and if you hadn't been so utterly astounded, you might have profited by it. Your grandma requires firm management.'

'She likes you,' you observed miserably. 'She wouldn't take it from me alone. I did try one day.'

'All these lessons in household management have been free and without obligation,' I cried with sudden passion, gripping your wrist. 'When have I ever demanded the slightest return? When have I indicated that you owed me anything? Or made indelicate suggestions? Or said or done the least thing that could not be positively flaunted before grandmothers far stricter than yours? Describe to me the occasions on which I have taken advantage of the position I have laboriously built up for myself in this house.'

You remained perfectly mute with terror. A puff of wind caused the shadows to stroke your face in a frenzy.

'Then open the gate and let me in!' I exclaimed in a strangled voice. 'I don't care to be kept waiting. I'm impatient by nature, though some people don't suspect it from my manner.'

As we approached the house, Mrs Strumbold cried: 'A little tiff! But never mind. What's for supper? At my age one has been reduced to essentials. Bolts on the door are quite superfluous.'

'Who said anything about doors?' you asked with horror. 'Besides, they are all open.'

I saw that you had capitulated. That you had resigned yourself into my power. The struggle was finally over. You realized as clearly as I did that it was useless to resist fate. We had been designed for each other from the very beginning. I had often explained this, but only now did you seem properly to take it in. Your eyes became immensely large, strange and green.

I stood on the hearthrug with my back to the fireplace. This was the best room and the remains of a chandelier swung from the ceiling. Many of the pendants had dropped off and the wiring for the electric candles was makeshift. A modern light with shade would have looked far better, but this chandelier proved that Mrs Strumbold once inhabited larger and more classy apartments. In the corner, for similar reasons, there was a huge Victorian desk. Though stained, scorched, chipped and scarred, it ranked as an heirloom. I surveyed these familiar objects with particular care, for I wished to stamp this evening on my memory for ever.

'How are you, Grandma?' I enquired genially of the crumpled figure watching from a chintz armchair. 'I think you're looking better tonight. Less pale. Less stiff. Younger! Certainly, a great deal. It's marvellous at your age.'

Her rodent glance flicked up to mine as she stated: 'There's nothing wrong with me except hunger and never has been. I was twisted in an accident in rough weather on board ship long ago.'

'You are so romantic,' I said, leaning slightly over her. 'A poor writer's dream. Do you know, I feel I'm going to talk about myself tonight. Of my hopes and aspirations, my plans for the future. The time has come for me to confide these things to you and Nancy. The atmosphere is right and I need your advice, your help,' I cried with a sudden tremor in my voice. 'Listen to me now. I've had much experience of the world, mostly disagreeable. Not that I complain. On the contrary, it will prove my fortune.'

She did not offer to interrupt my diatribe. A sardonic smile seemed to wrestle with the twitch in her right cheek. But I may have been mistaken.

I continued, for I could not stop, 'I feel at home here and that's a sensation I've seldom had. I left my parents very young because I couldn't bear them. They lived in a Yorkshire village and I'm urban by nature. The solitudes of the countryside oppress me. Sometimes I have nightmares where I'm walking in that village street again. There were forty houses and a medieval church recommended in the guide-books for its brasses. Every soul in the place was known to me. It was impossible to find privacy. They discovered one's very thoughts and if these differed from the accepted mould, one caught it. And there was nowhere to escape to except the awful empty fields on every side. The sheep, the cows, the bees, the sunset views, the leaves, the wind and rain were poetic enough, but they didn't stimulate me like a pavement full of jostling people, all totally unknown, flanked by huge buildings, composed of tiny rooms, densely inhabited. Only in such perfect anonymity can one find freedom.'

I looked down and was much relieved to see that Mrs Strumbold had not heard a word of my speech. Her attention was entirely fixed on the sounds from the kitchen indicating that supper was practically ready.

'Madam,' I cried, as gaily as I could. 'Dinner is served, I believe. Will you take my arm?' So speaking, I dragged her sharply up. This was the most economical way of getting her to her feet.

'Ha-ugh,' she gasped, tottering slightly. 'I'm glad of that.

I was afraid you might be going to talk all night from the sound of things.'

'I may do,' I replied, picking our way between the chairs, tables, stools, workbags, magazines and rucked-up mats impeding the path to the kitchen. 'Affairs have reached a turning-point....'

'Turn for the better, I hope,' she interrupted, screwing her neck and shoulders sideways in order to examine my face.

'Hold steady,' I said.

'I am steady,' she grumbled. 'Or would be if you weren't hanging on my arm. What d'you keep treating me like an old idiot for? I'm as much all there as ever I was.' She made blowing and grinding noises.

'It's a wonderful thing to be old,' I exclaimed with the utmost enthusiasm. 'You can't imagine how the subject fascinates me. I shall always be grateful to Nancy for having given me the opportunity to know you. My previous studies in old folk's homes and other places were cruelly curtailed by circumstances beyond my control. I'd hardly got started. That sort of research takes years, if it's to be properly done. I'd have liked to disguise myself as an old woman and move in amongst them. Because then I'd have found out what they spoke of when they were alone together; and how they behaved when they thought nobody was watching. I'd have pretended to be a deaf mute,' I muttered, squeezing the fragile arm in my grip while extraordinary sensations I could not exactly name coursed over me.

'Ah, my God,' you interrupted. 'What'll be the end of it?'

'The rubbish you do talk,' said Mrs Strumbold, lowering herself into her place. 'Let go, will you. How am I to hold the knife?'

I put the knife into her hand and pressed it. Silence fell because I was considering how best to proceed. I did not wish my future jeopardized by some stupidity. For the fact was that I was, at that moment, down and out. I couldn't sell any of my writings, though I knew them to be good. Other boys with newer names had caught the editors' fancy. They were interested in themes that I'd neglected and which turned out now to have news value. The old folk had become boring, for the time being at least. The morals, beliefs and general antics of the very young were all the rage. Being myself only recently past this stage of life, I hadn't the slightest interest in it. Adolescence had been for me a horrible experience, full of intractable problems, each enormously magnified by shyness, ignorance and general lack of elementary knowhow.

The very recollection was painful. I dismissed it and fixed my mind on present manœuvres. I was half-way through a novel which was certainly a masterpiece. I never felt so sure of anything in my life. I loved you, loved you, loved you. Far from being an obstacle, your appalling Grandma was an asset, as far as I was concerned. She increased my feeling for you to an amazing degree. The whole situation here in The Nook was a gold-mine. My half-novel was about the three of us, sufficiently transposed, of course. I thought I could spend a lifetime writing about The Nook. Crowds of ideas came into my head every time I passed through the front door. I'd never experienced such intense inspiration anywhere else.

'Art is an extraordinary thing!' I exclaimed without warning. 'You can't tell how it's going to take you. Suddenly one is stimulated by the most unlikely scenes and everything is different immediately. It has happened to me in station waiting-rooms and in low snackbars, strewn with cigarette ends and dirty bits of bread. The depressed crowd of all ages usually gathered in such places seem as if they must be waiting for some tremendous event. Perhaps they are. How can one say? The smells, the flies, the flaking paint, all add to one's expectation for reasons it is not possible to determine.'

'How your eyes shine,' you said apprehensively.

'Give me the saucepan,' said Mrs Strumbold. 'What was a cook like you doing in a snackbar, anyway?'

'Why go searching for bluebell glades at great trouble and expense?' I cried, leaning ardently towards you. 'I was once acquainted with a poet who made his living by means of rhymes on Christmas cards, for which he had an amazing facility. Twenty different quatrains in a morning were nothing to him. Yet, when it came to real poetry, as he called it, he had to be sitting on banks of thyme, or under beech trees, or beside purling brooks, to get any results. He spent a fortune on trains, buses, shoe leather and drinks in riverside hostelries hung with warming-pans.'

'Must have had plenty of time to spare,' said Mrs Strumbold, licking busily. A small blob of cheese sauce twitched up and down on her right cheek like a yellow insect dancing.

You sighed lingeringly, as if the soft coolness of bluebell woods suggested a haven of silence and peace.

'He was a criminal waster of time,' I said. 'For the banks of thyme were always covered with picnic parties long before he got there. The beech trees were full of kids climbing while their mums stood in the purling brooks washing out the thermoses. But at least the pubs had drinks in them, at a price. Naturally, one had to pay for historic atmosphere, as represented by the warming-pans; and for beauty, by which was meant the adjacent river.'

'I think the river is beautiful,' you sobbed. 'Especially in the evening.'

'Quite right,' I said, getting out my handkerchief and tenderly wiping your tears. 'It's just that I, personally, don't find it elevating. It's too relaxing, too dying-away and reminiscent of a thousand swooning ballads in vulgar magazines.'

'You must get your boyfriend to write a poem to me one day,' said Mrs Strumbold. 'I believe he'd do it very well if he let himself go.'

'It's a bargain!' I cried, opening a tin containing chocolate cake which I had ordered you to conceal until the right moment. 'Will you honour me, madam, by sampling a piece of this cake? I have entered it for a competition where the first prize is a motor car. Have some, Nancy darling. It'll do you good. I think most of your nervous troubles are due to insufficient nourishment.'

'It looks all right,' said the old cannibal with satisfaction. She had put on a pair of spectacles. 'I should like to be taken to a bluebell glade in a motor car.' She began munching and grunting.

'I may talk in a light way about art and inspiration,' I said, the chocolate-covered knife gripped in my hand, 'but that is in order not to bore you. Actually, it's the ruling passion of my life. I'm ready to sacrifice everything to it. How otherwise could I endure the poverty, loneliness and humiliations that I have done all these years? How could I keep my spirits up the way I do?'

'I keep mine up,' Mrs Strumbold remarked. 'Eighty-eight though I am and the sole survivor of a large family, except Nancy. Maybe I shall outlast her, too.'

'I dare say you will,' you whispered, your piece of cake lying on your plate, only faintly nibbled.

'Well, then,' I said, 'why don't we throw in our lot together?'

'No, no,' you protested in a muted shriek. 'I mean....'

'For God's sake, Nancy,' said Mrs Strumbold. 'Can't you recognize a good offer when you see one? You are going to marry her, I suppose,' she added, leering up at me, a sardonic smile mingling with the rim of chocolate round her lips.

'If she will permit me,' I said hurriedly. 'If she will honour me with the prospect of so much happiness. But I don't want to move in on false pretences. Let's have everything fair and above board.'

'Oh, have you got some woman somewhere?' said Mrs Strumbold. 'Shut up, Nancy. Let's get this straight before we go any further.'

You now slumped in your chair, staring at the bit of cake as if it were poisoned.

'No,' I said in what I hoped was a calm, seductive tone, 'Nancy is the only woman in my life. For various reasons, I've never loved anyone the way I do her. I haven't had the least inclination to tie myself up with anybody else. Darling, I didn't think it was possible for the human frame to long and to hunger as I have done. Judging from previous experience, that is to say.'

You blushed. Grandma remarked: 'I strongly advise you not to miss the opportunity, Nancy. I believe he will prove highly satisfactory in all respects.'

'Thank you, madam,' I said quickly, for I felt she might be going to add something less genial. 'I shall endeavour to live up to your opinion. Nancy has only to say the word and we'll be married as soon as the usual formalities allow. But she knows that and has done for ages. I don't wish to hurry her. She has her own idea of what's appropriate and I'm perfectly ready to fall in with it. Yet, there are other matters which cannot be similarly postponed, or I would do so, for it's painful to have to confess to misfortune. Have

55

you ever been acquainted with the acting profession, Mrs Strumbold?'

'I knew an actor once,' she stated shortly. 'He couldn't even cook.'

'Then you know that an artistic career is particularly subject to ups and downs. To periods,' I said vaguely, forgetting where I was as recollection crowded thickly, 'when one wonders how one will find strength to go on. Whether it is worth the time and effort required for even the most ephemeral creation. And the bad periods come on one without warning. Sometimes because inspiration has flagged and can't be revived by any of the usual methods employed in these fixes. Sometimes it's due to one's having been seized by such a tremendous idea that everything else is excluded from consciousness. In the latter case,' I continued in a casual voice, 'one finds it exceedingly difficult to concentrate on pieces for immediate sale. There is only one life to be had and why should one be obliged to waste it for lack of a little capital to tide one over a period of intense, superb, but not instantly productive work?'

I paused, overwhelmed by this sad picture of myself as a persecuted genius. But let it not be thought, darling, that I was making it up in order to impose myself on you and your grandma. I don't wish to go down to history as a shameless scrounger on two helpless women. For those unacquainted with Mrs Strumbold would be most likely to describe her thus, merely on account of her age. Oh, what a great advantage it is in this world to be immensely old and fierce. No, no, my sole object has always been to advance your happiness, sweetheart. I wanted to stand between you and Grandma; to enter your extraordinary family circumstances to the fullest extent. I felt certain that here was the necessary explosive force to fire a chain of masterpieces. I was determined to test the hypothesis thoroughly.

'I've half a novel done which I'm positive will make all our fortunes for ever!' I cried with the utmost conviction. 'Think of films, serials, television rights, translations, book club editions, paperbacks, school reprints, etc. Nowadays, there's a vast overseas market for anything successful. No one, white or black, in the distant parts of the world can endure to be left behind in the culture race. Nobody is going to be called "backward" in these glorious times when the colonialist yoke has everywhere been thrown off with contumely. When the white man's superiority has been decisively disproved. When the battle for entry to exclusive clubs, swimming-pools, beaches, hotels and reserved compartments of all sorts has reached a climax, even among persons three-quarters naked and supposedly ignorant of current events. This vast audience,' I said to Mrs Strumbold, 'will buy my novel, when completed.'

'Hurr-rupp,' she replied from her dreams. She had sagged right down in her chair and resembled a heap of old clothes. Her head was tipped over her shoulder, her mouth half open.

'Wake up! Wake up!' I exclaimed, shaking her in a frenzy. 'Our future's at stake. I can't finish my book without your help because I'm destitute. I've been kicked out by an illiterate landlady for lack of a few pounds. Am I to bed down in a ditch with the tramps, Irishmen, gipsies, crooks and drunks by whom secluded fields and copses are infested?'

'Let go of me,' said Mrs Strumbold. 'I heard you. Why shouldn't I take forty winks at my age? There was plenty of time while you got to the point. Now what is it? I'm not lending you a penny, genius or no genius, ditch or no ditch.' She stared at me morosely. You began to tremble.

'Lend me a penny?' I said with as much indignation as seemed politic. 'What's this? I should hope not, indeed.

You misunderstand me. I was just coming to my proposals, which are not at all of the kind you suspect.'

'I thought you said you were bankrupt,' she remarked, yawning tremendously. 'Excuse me. Can't help it. Feel so comfortable inside.'

'So I am,' I rejoined, 'but only as far as cash is concerned. And that's temporary. I'm expecting payment any day for an article on health and beauty. It's been accepted and the price negotiated, though they won't cough up till actual publication. How am I to tell,' I cried in momentary despair, 'whether it will please them to print my contribution in the next issue, or the one after, or perhaps months ahead? It depends on what goes on among the princes of Arabia, the Russians, Chinese, Americans; what natural disasters may occur, earthquakes, for instance, where whole villages are swallowed up to the immediate benefit of newshounds. Health and beauty, being always topical, may be indefinitely postponed, if space is tight.'

'Maybe it will,' said Mrs Strumbold, her little eyes three-quarters shut. 'I never read about health and beauty myself. I leave it to Nancy.'

'All these things mean,' I rushed on, dodging your apprehensive stare, 'that new arrangements are necessary to enable me to continue my profession. I must find a place to live where I can be of use in practical ways, not in order to avoid rent, but simply so as to put off payment until the better days dawn. There is something about you and Nancy, Mrs Strumbold, that makes me certain my luck has changed. I feel it very fervently and I beg you to give me a trial as a lodger. Name your own price. I'll do all the cooking and endeavour to entertain you into the bargain.' I stopped for lack of breath, though there was more, far more, I might have said in extenuation of my claims.

'Why couldn't you have said this straight out?'

grumbled the old woman. 'Making me listen to all that palaver. Interrupting my forty winks long before it was necessary.'

'He can't come! He can't come!' you screamed in hopeless protest. 'He's got to take me out of this, not move in.'

Mrs Strumbold threw a glass of water at you, remarking with contempt: 'Her mother was just the same. No sense.' She filled up another glass with unusual agility, considering the misshapen condition of her hands.

'Hush, darling,' I cried, leaping to your defence and mopping your head with a tea towel. 'I'm only trying to do what's best for both of us. How can I take you away when we've nowhere to go? Besides, what about Grandma? She can't be abandoned just like that.'

'I should think not,' interpolated Mrs Strumbold, glass at the ready.

'One has duties. One has obligations,' I continued loudly. 'There are things one can't do if one is to retain one's self-respect.'

'What self-respect?' you yelled, drumming on the table with your fists so that all the knives and forks chattered together.

'Better try another go of water,' said Mrs Strumbold. 'It's quicker in the end. Two or three glasses used to settle her mother nicely.' A reminiscent grin curved the edges of her mouth.

'I guarantee to improve Grandma out of all recognition,' I murmured into your ear. 'I believe she suffers from boredom as much as anything. With interesting meals and outings along the towpath to see the sights, I believe she'd be a great deal sweeter when you got back in the evening. I always write best at five o'clock in the morning. It's a quiet dead time that stimulates me. So I'd easily be able to fit in plenty of entertainment for Grandma later in the day. And I would, too. I swear it. My whole object is to further your happiness, even at the risk of my own advancement. Give it a trial. Give me a chance. If it doesn't work we'll make other plans. Circumstances will change. Money will come in and we'll be free.'

'What's all this whispering?' Mrs Strumbold demanded suspiciously. 'I said he could come, didn't I? Don't be such a fool, Nancy. He's by far the most promising boyfriend you've ever had. The others seemed to fade away after a couple of visits,' she added to me. 'I don't know why. I'm sure I did my best to be polite and welcoming, even though they weren't up to much. I've been a woman of the world in my time and I know how to talk to people, no matter who they are. High up, or low down. Half-witted, or clever. You settle for this one, Nancy, and we'll neither of us regret it. I can't stay and look after you for ever. Who's going to see to things when I'm gone if you don't fix yourself up decently? Heavens above, the things a grandmother is expected to arrange these days.'

'You see, sweetheart,' I cried exultingly. 'Everything's decided. It's fate. Dry your eyes. You'll not regret it. Ah, if you would only trust me. What experiences you must have had with previous boyfriends to make you so shy and unsteady. All my possessions are in a sack at the bus station. I'll run and fetch them now.'

9

T H U S the three of us began our new life together, Joseph wrote deliriously. I returned with the sack as fast as I possibly could and you showed me up to this room. I didn't enquire what Mrs Strumbold had said during my absence. She reminded me of a boa constrictor I had once seen in a zoo just after it had swallowed a whole carcass at one gulp. I shall never forget the happiness of that first wakeful night, lying on the damp mattress, listening to you muttering in your sleep on one side of me and Grandma powerfully snoring on the other.

At times, I wondered whether this muttering was coming from your dreams; or whether you were really wide awake, protesting. Not that you had anything to fear. All my arrangements had been thought out with a careful view to your comfort and convenience. I knew I wasn't a cruel man. My conscience was clear. I had offered you the position of wife to a rising genius and, for your own sake, could not allow you to refuse merely on account of some nervous flutter, some unaccountable shrinking from life which perhaps could best be described by a psychiatrist. I mean, more scientifically. I myself intended to give a complete explanation for the lay reader.

'My treasure!' he cried, jumping up and staring sharply into the mirror, as if in the hope of catching sight of another face. Then he turned quickly round and searched the room behind him. Everything was in its usual place and he seemed to remember having left the door slightly ajar. Indeed, he must have done so, otherwise it would be shut.

'But never mind all that,' he murmured, rumpling up his hair. 'You know I should adore it if you came back to haunt me. I once went to a seance just to see what it was like. Why is the next world so largely inhabited by Red Indians? All the spirits conjured up were of that nation. Are those the sort of people you consort with now, darling? Have you replaced me with a coloured gentleman? I ask only out of curiosity and not in the least from racial prejudice. I'm a little anxious on your account, that's all. You were never quite at ease with anyone dark.' A triumphant look settled on his face.

'Nancy, Nancy, Nancy!' he sang in a high-pitched voice that fluted through the empty rooms, the doors of which were every one ajar today. 'Do you remember the time when we danced, waltzing round the table until we couldn't bear Mrs Strumbold's laughter any more? There was something so grim and scornful about it that the world seemed to be demolished, leaving us standing on an awful edge.'

He began circling on his toes, his arms stretched out as if embracing a partner and humming those parts of the old tune his memory still held. The rain was very furious today, driving in great swathes over the roofs, travelling on an icy wind that froze the people under their umbrellas, which, seen from above, were like the shining backs of beetles scurrying to their holes. The last leaves fell on top of them, sticking here and there, red, yellow, brown and russet patterns on the moving backs.

Joseph danced down the stairs, singing incoherently. He didn't think he had really got the tune right. 'Surely, darling, it must have had quite a gay rhythm, or we would not have been carried away by it in the first place. This is more like a dirge.'

A certain pungent smell drifted through the open doors from the sheeted furniture, presumably, and the cupboards spilling papers in great heaps and petrified cascades. He recognized it immediately as the smell given off by Mrs Strumbold during her last years.

How we were enfolded by it, he meditated, gliding through the hall. It even got into our underclothes and no amount of washing and hanging out in gales ever quite removed it. He remembered exactly the way their vests used to flap on the line, tugging at the pegs and tangling together on these occasions. But you didn't seem to take up the idea of underclothes with much enthusiasm, he hummed, skirting round a shadow that stretched a thin arm through the sitting-room door. But then, enthusiasm was never much in your line.

Outside the kitchen window, he saw a man with a box of groceries in his arms. As the rain was pouring fiercely down on sugar, butter, breakfast food and matches, he opened the back door, saying pleasantly: 'Put them on the table, will you? This is no weather for hanging about in gardens, even well-cut well-trimmed and carefully cultured plots, let alone a wilderness like mine.'

'Cor, you said it,' replied the man, placing the sodden box on the table. 'Real wicked it is. Got stuck down Stubble Green way this morning. Thought I'd never get the van out, the mud was that thick. Yeah, all the streams is full up already and November 'ardly started.' He leaned against the cooker, staring curiously at Joseph and into the house behind him. Water dripped in a circle round his feet from the skirts of his macintosh.

'What's the date?' asked Joseph intently.

'Sixth of November,' answered Toby the vanman, his

manner becoming more and more familiar every second. 'Didn't you 'ear no fireworks last night? Not but what most of them wouldn't go off. The kiddies wasn't 'alf disappointed. The catherine wheels was a complete washout. So was the Roman candles. I did get the rockets started by 'olding an umbrella over them while the fuse was lighting. But the wind blew them into the trees. What a year! It'll end up in a flood, you mark my words. The ground's that soaked it can't take no more and the river's 'alfway up the bank, even though they've drawed the weir.'

As the man chattered on, his guttural accent filling up the room with unaccustomed sound, Joseph was reflecting: Maybe those bangs I heard yesterday were fireworks. If so, it throws an entirely new light on everything. For it is scarcely possible, darling, that you would choose to haunt me through the medium of children's rockets. You were always so conventional, I mean. If those noises were the explosion of toy rockets, crackers and jumping jacks, you cannot have had anything to do with them. It must have been due to my imagination, and to intense longing to hear from you that made me think there was hammering on the roof. Like a person trying to get in. But you know where the doors are as well as I do.

'At what hour,' he asked his visitor politely, 'does a family man like yourself let off fireworks? How long do the festivities last? Not that I wish to intrude on your private habits. Don't think it. I'm against interference in any form.'

'Soon as it gets dark. The kids won't wait no more,' replied Toby, goggle-eyed. He'd just noticed that this cove was wearing a necklace of blue beads. Otherwise, he was dressed as a man. But there were those for whom the underclothes were enough. There'd been an epidemic of stealing from clothes lines in the district lately. The wife had lost two pairs of knickers, hung out at night for modesty's sake.

'It's hardly likely, then, that any noise occurring at, say, midnight, would be due to these celebrations,' Joseph remarked, slipping the necklace into his pocket as he spoke. It was one Mrs Strumbold had been accustomed to lend her granddaughter for special occasions. The smell of the old woman was now very strong, as if it had slid along the floor on a draught and suddenly spiralled five feet eight inches into the air. This was Joseph's height. Toby, however, did not appear to notice anything unusual. Perhaps because he kept his mouth open and breathed mainly through it; or lack of education prevented him from interpreting the evidence of his senses; or bad smells were such a natural concomitant of his life that he expected them everywhere. Joseph would have preferred to settle the question finally, one way or the other, but did not see how it could be done without giving explanations to which this person had no right. I have always been careful of your susceptibilities, darling, he silently apostrophized his ghost. You must grant me that, at least.

'So you think there'll be a flood?' he asked, wondering why he tried to detain anyone as thoroughly uncongenial as a grocer's assistant.

'Yeah, bound to be,' said Toby with relish.

'It's set in for a real wet winter. We 'aven't 'ad one for five years, neither. It's got to come some time. Stands to reason.'

He had good ears and kept them pricked for distant sounds, such as creaking boards, closing doors, suppressed titters and other noises one would expect to hear in a house of vice. For it was rumoured that the most amazing orgies took place here, the participants arriving at two or three o'clock in the morning and staying in the upstairs rooms for days, finally departing again in the small hours. There were people who swore that the lights were on all night; that a certain sort of dances were held — they had heard the music; that some performers were specially chosen for age and ugliness and others for exteme youth and delicate physique; that because Joseph was well known and rich, though a miser, he had bribed the police to leave him alone. It was enough to turn a bloke socialist, some said. 'What's the entrance fee?' said others. 'Let's gatecrash,' said the drunkest round the bar. But no one ever followed up this suggestion, though it appealed immensely to all present. No one knew how these rumours had first started.

Joseph unpacked the box, laying the contents out in neat rows on the table in order to minimize the effects of damp. Perhaps he ought to light an oil stove. A bit of warmth in the house would mitigate the sepulchral atmosphere. He was anxious to cheer up sufficiently to be able to cast a happy glow over his prose. How otherwise could his great memorial reflect the extraordinary joys he had experienced here in The Nook? He would certainly light the stove, which was a round one with a perforated top that cast a most delightful pattern on the ceiling after dark.

At this point he remembered the vanman's presence. The oaf was propped against the cooker in a listening attitude, a sly grin on his rubber mouth, his suet eyes wide open. Not that he's entirely unattractive, Joseph thought. I can imagine some people finding him quite fetching. But not me and not now. No time. Out.

He advanced cautiously on his opponent, since he was large and tolerably strong, saying: 'I believe the rain is easing off for a moment. I think if you were to run for it you'd reach your van not very much wetter. It's a great mistake to let opportunities slip in this life. That's my advice to you, speaking as an older man and one experienced in vicissitude.' He was close up against the fellow, muttering into his damp and grimy face. The smell of Mrs Strumbold was making him feel drunk. He began to wonder what he was saying and whether it was entirely wise: 'Not that I complain of my lot. On the contrary, my God, I feel myself singled out for special favour. I once said something of the sort on the wireless and it was wrongly taken up by the interviewer. He thought I meant religion. But it was only a manner of speech. How can one believe in the Almighty in this day and age? The very idea is insulting to an educated person. You'd better go, my man, or you'll regret it.'

Astonishment had almost deprived Toby of the use of his feet. It had simply never occurred to him that prolonged debauchery — the very idea set him tingling — could affect one in the head.

'Darling,' cried Joseph, slamming the door at last behind his obnoxious friend, 'why do we allow nonsensical people like him to engage our attention? To fritter away the short period we have left together? For how can I tell for certain whether I shall later join you in some marvellous empyrean inhabited chiefly by Red Indians?'

He seized his pen and, hardly thinking what he did, began to write.

IO

You went creeping down the path towards the bus stop. I could see you intermittently between the bushes, trees, lamp-posts, road signs, obstructing the view from the sitting-room window. I had kissed you very passionately on the doorstep, saying: 'Darling, why worry if you didn't enjoy it quite so much as you expected? It's a most usual reaction, I assure you. Love is a thing which has to be learnt and practised in order to bring out its full bouquet. Think of that! Think of the pleasures that will certainly be ours in a few months' time when we are less clumsy, less shy and have discovered the things that it really suits us to do. It's a matter of experiment. I've read a great number of books on the subject and I know what I'm talking about. Not dirty books, sweetheart. Please don't imagine that. No, no, on the contrary. I borrowed them from a learned library of which I was a member in my palmy days when I could afford the subscription. They were marked: For distribution to the medical profession only. All possibilities were described without circumlocution and with perfect decency. Is it right that these revealing and essential volumes should be restricted to doctors and members of learned libraries? But that's entirely by the way. I only mention the fact in order to set your mind at rest. Don't worry, my love. We are on the brink of the most marvellous happiness.'

When I had delivered this speech, at top speed since the

bus was expected very shortly, I bit the lobe of your ear and it blushed the most beautiful red I ever saw in my life. Instead of being uplifted by my inspired discourse, however, you gave me a look of the greatest horror and slunk towards the gate. This puzzled me a good deal, in spite of my vast reading, I admit. For you had been wide awake and waiting for me when I came. You were ready naked and not in the least surprised to find me standing by your bed in the same state. Could a man like me have done anything at all in the absence of a definite response? I knew the answer to that, at least, without having to look it up among the many chapters, sections, subheadings, footnotes and endless paraphernalia of scientific dissertations. I hoped very much that you hadn't contracted some obscure guilt complex; for the descriptions of these I had found immensely boring and contradictory. They tended to send me to sleep and, in short, I was ill-informed on that aspect and didn't know quite what counter-steps to take.

'Never mind, sweetest,' I cried through the window, though you were now too far off to hear. 'It's only a matter of saving up until I can re-join that library. They have all the answers there. People don't realize what fundamental activities reading and writing are. Where is a bookworm if not at the centre of life and experience? Burrowing and burrowing into the heart of things.' I felt a tremendous rush of excitement. I was still young enough to think that time was mine and could be used to further my own ends.

I hurried into the kitchen to prepare Mrs Strumbold's breakfast. She liked coffee, porridge, eggs, sausages, toast, marmalade and anything else she could get. Fortunately, she preferred it on a tray in bed. This gave us a chance to have our first meal in privacy. It was a perfect arrangement. I sang and whistled as I worked. Mrs Strumbold thumped on the floor overhead encouragingly.

I composed an impromptu song about you, relating ridiculous imaginary adventures on the bus as you journeyed to the office. Your boss was a woman, so I was spared any jealousy there. She was a very tough, severe sort of boss, you told me. Men were terrified of her. She employed only girls. Some of these were her favourites, small under-queens in the hierarchy. The rest either hoped to reach this rank, or contemplated giving notice. I advised you not to leave, as the wages were better than you could have obtained elsewhere. That was how this bossess kept her business always fully staffed and, at the same time, indulged a capricious temper.

My voice soared lightly above the rattle of Mrs Strumbold's plate and cup, her knives, forks, spoons and various containers for butter, salt, sugar, pepper and mustard. The tray was rather dented and the things inclined to slide together in the middle of it as I climbed the stairs.

'Good morning,' I sang. 'It's a wonderful day. I believe the sun's going to come out almost at once. Everything conspires to our content.' I began drawing the curtains.

The sudden grey light revealed Mrs Strumbold lying flat on her back, her eyes wide open, her hair elaborately screwed up with curlers. Her teeth were grinning through a glass of water on the table. I handed them to her and, having flicked them very dexterously into her mouth, she said: 'Is that a quotation?'

'No,' I replied frankly, 'my memory is too poor. But, naturally, it has been inspired by the many years of wide reading in which I have persevered, despite every obstacle.' So speaking, I seized her bedjacket in one hand and the pillows in the other. In a trice, I had her reclining at a proper angle for the breakfast tray.

'Wah-hup,' she gasped as I wedged her firmly. 'Ask me

70

for a reference any time you want a job as nurse-companion.' She leered in a provoking way.

'I hope you slept well,' I said, placing the tray on top of her. She sagged a little under the weight.

'The slightest noise wakes me,' she remarked indifferently, taking the cover off the central plate and curling her fingers round the knife and fork. 'Doors opening and closing, for instance. Whispering. Creaking. Tittering under blankets. It's my age, I suppose. I put it down to that, at least.'

'How interesting,' I said. 'May I help you to some salt?'

'You can,' she stated, 'and pepper.'

I peppered her sausages very liberally for I was nervous of what she might say next. Suppose she thought it necessary to put on sanctimonious airs? Suppose I were suddenly to find myself in the gutter again without a roof, a penny, or any prospect of being able to finish my novel concerning a young man, flattened at an early age by a diabolical grandmother? I felt certain I had struck a rich vein here, perhaps the best it ever would be my fortune to discover.

Then there was you who were quite essential to my well-being, without which I would find it difficult to continue to write. An artist has to be careful in so many different ways. I was sure everything would turn out splendidly for all three of us if I were only granted time to get properly started. Time, time, I prayed, while the pepper pot trembled in my hand and a brown dust settled on the breakfast tray.

'Atishoo!' said Mrs Strumbold. 'Are you trying to blow my head off, or what? Stop it, I tell you. You're ruining my food.'

'Forgive me,' I cried, immediately desisting. 'I hardly know what I'm doing for some reason. I suffer from apprehensive fits, you know. I believe it's connected with my being an intellectual.'

'Rubbish,' said Mrs Strumbold.

'But if it's not that,' I stammered, 'how am I to deal with it? If my troubles cannot be resolved by my joining a learned library and looking up the answers, I am lost. Because I have no other way of coping. Because I cannot imagine a life without the aid of books and all the worlds on worlds that they contain. You are not sufficiently a reader to follow my meaning, even were I to explain at enormous length, which I don't propose to do. I am at least sophisticated enough to know what's fitting in a house like this.'

'You flatter yourself,' she remarked. 'Have you ever been to bed with anyone before? I thought not.'

'But doesn't that prove my essential respectability?' I murmured in despair. 'My honesty and refusal to take cheap satisfaction instead of the real thing?'

'No, it doesn't,' she said, spooning marmalade liberally on to her toast. 'It shows you're not normal. Nor's Nancy.'

I suddenly felt rather faint and sat down on the end of the bed, my hands clasped tightly together on my knees. I could hardly believe my own ears when I heard myself say in a dignified, reasonable tone: 'I think, madam, that you might give me some credit for decent feeling. Just because I'm not in the habit of jumping in and out of bed with all comers, it doesn't mean that I lack the usual urges of mankind. On the contrary, they are the stronger in me for being bottled up. Also, you know perfectly well that it was my wish to marry Nancy before our honeymoon. It is in deference only to her desire that the ceremony has been postponed.'

'All right. I believe you,' said Mrs Strumbold peering

into her cup. 'Is that pepper floating on the top? I can't see properly without my glasses.'

'I don't think so,' I said, skimming it with a teaspoon. 'Not much anyway.' I leaned back against the bedpost full of the most dismal sensations. What if I was not wicked enough to pass muster with Mrs Strumbold? She was watching me with extraordinary avidity and I was again struck by her cannibalistic air. She drank her coffee as if it was blood. My blood, I thought. Nancy's got none left.

Nervous excitement made me chatter: 'What you need is a man about the house. On account of my extensive reading, and also the many vicissitudes I have suffered, with which I have not scrupled to bore you, I have adapted myself with considerable success to the necessities of every-day life.'

'Ah,' said Mrs Strumbold, taking one of the curlers out of her hair. 'Hand me the mirror, will you?'

'Though possessed of the temperament of an artist, I'm easy to get on with. It's true I'm completely wrapped up in my own work and ambitions, yet I take trouble with my fellows and comport myself in a genial manner, on the whole. I don't wish to sing my own praises to excess, or to seem smug, but why shouldn't I have my due? Why should I be perpetually numbered amongst the lowest of the low — that is to say the poor and those not generally trusted with large sums of money in case the strain should prove too much for them?'

Mrs Strumbold was combing out her curls with great concentration. I got up and leaned against the window frame, looking out and speaking rapidly: 'I have resolved to end that period of my life with your help. With Nancy's. I once knew a man who had a loyal and tender family. Even uncles, aunts and cousins stood by when he was in difficulties.'

73

'Free meals, I suppose,' interpolated Mrs Strumbold absently. 'Bed and board gratis.' She squinted at her profile in the mirror.

'What was the result?' I cried loudly. 'Why, he succeeded in his profession and paid for them in their old age. He found the most lovely home by the seaside. There was hot and cold water at all hours of the day, a varied diet and a matron specially picked for patience and sympathy. Rules were kept to the minimum. I read the brochure myself. Once a week they were allowed to sit up late. On Wednesday afternoons, they were taken to a concert on the promenade.'

'Sounds heavenly,' said Mrs Strumbold. 'I believe I would be an ornament to a place like that.'

I tried to imagine the malignant old person before me sitting in a rose garden with a rug over her knees and an indeterminate piece of knitting in her hands. This had been one of the photographs in the brochure so proudly shown me by my friend. It proved, he said, that his relatives had been most wise to invest their money in him. For what with the fall in the value of the pound and the fact that they were unexpectedly long-lived, their original capital would never have sufficed for these comforts. Whereas he, being able to lay out substantial sums at the right moment, through their kindness and foresight, had trebled their combined fortunes before you could say how do you do.

These things he had related to me in the lounge of an expensive hotel where he gave me a glass of sherry and his best wishes for my future prosperity. He would not insult me, he said, by offering a loan, because his business commitments happened to be at that particular stage where he could dispose of only such trivial amounts as it would degrade us both to mention, having regard to our old friend-

74

ship and the many misfortunes we had passed through together. He would have elaborated this theme, I felt sure, to my advantage, but a page boy came and whispered in his ear and he had to hurry away. Someone in Valparaiso wanted to speak to him on the telephone, he explained.

I stared gloomily at Mrs Strumbold. For there were times when my spirit wearied and I wondered whether I had really made the smart bargain I had supposed in the beginning. True, I was not starving, wet, cold, ragged or dirty. I had been provided with the theme for any number of books. But I was getting on only very slowly with the first volume in the projected series of masterpieces treating of old age, decrepitude, madness, death and similar best-selling subjects. Because this old cannibal was drinking my blood.

Mrs Strumbold had taken a piece of red ribbon from under her pillow and tied it round three large curls on the top of her head. 'Nobody seems to have any vitality nowadays,' she remarked. 'Why, when I was young we knew what we wanted and how to do it. We only had to have help much later on. Open the top right-hand drawer of the dressing-table.'

'There's nothing in it except a key,' I said, disappointed. From her manner, I had expected something rather different.

'It belongs to the box in the wardrobe,' she said.

An immense quantity of old coats, dresses, boots, shoes, wigs, umbrellas and corsets tumbled out as I opened the door. Some of these garments had been brightly coloured and sewn with glass beads, tinsel and gold thread here and there. They had the remains of artificial roses and carnations pinned to them. The wigs were all curly blacks, reds and blonds. Many bottles of cheap scent must have been poured over them at one time.

'The box is underneath,' said Mrs Strumbold.

'What's all this?' I exclaimed with horror. 'Why, I'm up to my knees in it. How will I ever get them in again? Oughtn't they to have mothballs? Why have you collected them? Such terrible scent.' I stepped back, but several of the dresses and three wigs had attached themselves to the various buttons on my clothes.

'Heh, heh, heh, ug-heh,' laughed Mrs Strumbold, the red ribbon trembling in her curls, the empty plates chattering together on the dented tray beside her. 'They're for dressing up. What else did you think?'

I was now struggling to unhook myself. Whichever way I twisted, tarnished gold thread and loops of false pearls seemed to result in my being more inextricably entangled. 'Dressing up as what?' I muttered at random. 'Hermaphrodites? Some of these wigs might be worn by men or women. And that which I took for a blouse I now see is a fancy waistcoat.'

'Never mind about all that,' cried Mrs Strumbold impatiently. 'The box is far more interesting.'

I delved into the bottom of the wardrobe where many pairs of gloves were lying, made of various materials. There were also parasols and bunches of feathers which might once have been hats, though it was impossible to be sure. Perhaps they were the remains of boas or decorations for vanished evening gowns and cloaks. All these I threw out into the room in a frenzy. They flew in semi-circles through the air, scattering dust and mould. Some disintegrated during the passage.

'Easy does it,' Mrs Strumbold remarked pleasantly as a shoe covered with sequins hit the tray; and something I had taken for another wig, but proved to be a false beard, lodged precariously on top of the glass of water in which she had just finished rinsing her teeth. 'It's lovely to see old possessions again. I'd quite forgotten that dress you've got in your hand now. Hold it up so I can look at it properly.'

Panting and covered with sweat and dirt, I stood in the middle of the heap and held up the dress in front of me.

'I believe it would suit you down to the ground,' she continued. 'I last wore it forty years ago.' She touched her curls and simpered slightly.

'Why a false beard?' I asked dreamily, leaning on the corner of the cupboard, the dress still clutched before me. 'It's so long since my finances were sufficiently buoyant to support the subscription to that wonderful library. I can't remember half the things I read. Some people imagine heaven as a place inlaid with gold and precious stones, the many mansions ringing with celestial song. Or else the music of the spheres. But if you can have music and architecture, why not literature? Think of the wonders that would be contained in a supernatural library! The marvels daily disclosed. The secrets uncovered, each one more extraordinary than the last. The thoughts set whirling in one's head. Eternity would pass in a flash. It is my considered opinion that the life of a ghost is one to be envied.'

'Isn't that the edge of the box under those slippers?' asked Mrs Strumbold, craning from the bed. She had put on her spectacles.

I dragged it out and she fitted the key into the lock, which proved very stiff, owing to age, rust, fluff and a course of bad treatment it had evidently received at one time. I could see scratches round it. The lid had had part of its imitation crocodile covering torn off. Mrs Strumbold wrestled intently. The ribbon had slipped in her hair. I was convinced that she did not regard me as a wicked schemer who had insinuated himself into the house with the object of seducing her granddaughter and thus securing an infinity of free board and lodging. No, it was much worse. She thought me a miserable little innocent; a namby-pamby; just the sort of ridiculous boyfriend one would expect Nancy to bring home.

'Libraries!' she snorted. 'Reading! What you need is practical instruction.'

I gazed at her sadly. In spite of my ambitions, I was full of ideals at that time. For I had a feeling that one oughtn't to be self-seeking and an egoist unless it were excused by the pursuit of higher ends. Thus, I was continually reminding myself — and you too, darling — of how useful my presence in the house was; how even Grandma would soon become feeble and require someone to look after her while you were working; how I was prepared to do this essential job free for as long as it should prove necessary.

'Eighty-eight's nothing,' I reminded you. 'She might last to a hundred and eight with her vitality.' The idea rendered you speechless and I also was rather staggered to have the problem expressed in actual numbers like that. But I recovered and pressed on with my self-justification.

I pointed out, in succinct phrases carefully rehearsed, that my masterpiece would be finished within six months and published a year after. So that, in eighteen months' time I would be rich, well known or, at least, well on the way to it. I swore to repay you a hundredfold for any inconvenience I might have caused. The plain fact was that your wages were scarcely enough to go round without two or three nights working late in the week. There were days when I thought I might have to take something temporary myself. The objection to this course was that it would put off the millennium indefinitely. You agreed, but in such a tired, indifferent way that I was quite miserable.

'I mustn't be deflected from my goal,' I said loudly and

suddenly. 'I owe it to Nancy. I've got to succeed. What does it matter if the many tasks I have to perform in your service, madam, are almost too much for me when combined with the strain of artistic creation? These trials are all for my good, I am sure. It is necessary to triumph over difficulties in order fully to develop one's personality. Think of the famous men of history. Had they a smooth passage from the word go? Napoleon? Shakespeare? Wellington? Michelangelo? Hitler?'

'Get your fingers under the edge of this lid,' gasped Mrs Strumbold, breathless from continual struggle with the lock. 'Give it a good jerk while I turn the key.'

'I think the handle of the fork would be better,' I suggested, picking it up and inserting it into the crack.

The box flew open and dozens of dirty postcards tumbled on to the bed. Some slid off and lodged among the piles of clothes now carpeting the floor.

'My husband's collection,' said Mrs Strumbold reminiscently. 'The best and most expensive to be had in Port Said and Alexandria. He never bothered with the ordinary tourist stuff.'

I picked up one or two. They were certainly very fine, of their kind, far surpassing anything obtainable in Soho. They illustrated with remarkable aptness many of the chapters I had read in the books addressed to the medical profession. Only here the slant was far from scientific. As I examined them, sitting on the end of Mrs Strumbold's bed, I reflected in general terms on the great difference there was between a subject treated in an abstract, clinical manner and the same material viewed strictly from an emotional, uneducated standpoint. I felt useful lessons in literary composition could be developed from this thought. I did not see what other moral could possibly be drawn from such pictures. The books had shown me how to approach things decently and I'd no intention of imitating the vulgarities depicted in these postcards, which I continued to pick up off Mrs Strumbold's recumbent form purely from intellectual curiosity.

'Good, aren't they?' said she with animation. 'Why ruin your eyes with pages of small print when you can get it at a glance like this?'

'I enjoy reading as an occupation,' I said as calmly as I could. 'The impact being less immediate, it gives one time to form a considered judgement. It develops the mind in a way that pictures cannot do, because to look at an object requires no concentration.'

'Too much reading addles the brains,' said Mrs Strumbold. 'My husband never read anything except Conrad. He knew those seas and all the islands. Those were wonderful days, before Nancy was ever thought of. We had our own boat and sailed wherever there was trade. We did what we liked.' She glanced round the room and at me with the utmost contempt.

'Madam!' I cried with sudden uncontrollable excitement. 'You are the most extraordinary individual I have ever met. Take me on as your pupil. Teach me what you know. I believe that if you and all your knowledge were to be enshrined in literature, it would redound to the benefit of the human race. At any rate, it would sell like wildfire and we would be rich. And famous. Don't you want to be famous?'

'Not specially,' said she, peering at a poor man being tortured.

'How amazing,' I replied, staggered. 'How original. How I differ from you there. But never mind. I shall observe you, whether you like it or not. After all, I'm owed something for the many uncomplaining services I perform. It's sheer dishonesty and sharp practice to pretend that free board and lodging are sufficient payment. Would a maid, or housekeeper, work without wages?'

'No, of course not,' she said. 'That's why I don't have one. Have you got the homosexuals down your end?'

I handed her a few, continuing: 'I'm too modest. That's my trouble. I once knew an advertising man and he was of the same opinion. Only persons to whom conceit came naturally, he said, succeeded in this life. One must study to make more than the best of oneself. The art could easily be learnt, he said, and promised to instruct me. But, unfortunately, he was called to America almost immediately on an important consultative job and I heard no more of him, though I wrote several letters of enquiry.'

'Modest?' said Mrs Strumbold. 'Prudish, I should have thought.' She waved a picture of a poor woman covered with blood.

All at once, I felt frightened. I ought to have taken your advice and fled with you from this appalling old image, novel or no novel. 'What does it matter if one is a little naïve?' I cried in a trembling voice. 'It's a virtue and can be made use of, like being abstemious, or truthful, or generous to those in distress. Very good books have often been written in which such ideas and qualities have been extolled.'

'Oh, tracts,' yawned Mrs Strumbold, both hands full of postcards. She had tied a spangled scarf in an enormous bow round her neck.

'Not only that, but people have actually profited from reading them. Even persons habitually moving in sophisticated circles.'

'Stuff and nonsense,' said Mrs Strumbold sleepily.

'Yes,' I insisted, overcome by strange revulsions which impelled me to make these ridiculous statements. 'They have confessed as much to me. I have been the recipient of the most surprising confidences. Lewd persons, especially, have related their adventures just because they sensed my fundamental decency. They wished to shock me and they did, though I tried not to show it out of pride, you know, and a feeling that one ought to be broadminded. But, more than once, I wondered whether they were really as bad as they made out. Whether they were telling me their dreams and the fancies that came to them at the end of an unsatisfactory day. Why are there always so many unsatisfactory days? Why is one inadequate in spite of all one's efforts? In spite of labours prolonged year in year out and growing more intense as time passes, sliding by without a halt and leaving footprints on one's hair and skin? I don't speak of the mind; for who can say whether that gets older or not? It grows larger, certainly, and stacked with items like a shop where no one ever comes to buy. And the goods are subject to a mysterious law of multiplication. They reach the ceiling. The counter disappears. The door is blocked. No one can get in. The owner is imprisoned. What am I saying?' I cried in despair.

Mrs Strumbold was heavily asleep. The covering of filthy postcards under which she lay rose lightly with her snores and sank again. Two fell off into the heap of tarnished finery beside the bed. I thought of shutting the cupboard and kicking the clothes under it. Also of stuffing the postcards back into the box. Also of cutting her throat as she lay there with her chin tilted conveniently upwards.

But I did not do any of these sensible things. No, I took up the tray full of dirty crockery, very gently and slowly in order to prevent sliding, rattling, crashing, or any sort of sharp noises that might disturb an old woman's dreams. I crept out of that disgraceful room on tiptoe and closed the door behind me like a sigh.

II

THAT was how I betrayed us both, my darling, wrote
Joseph largely and decisively across the page. He under-
lined the words. How much wiser you were than I ever
suspected at that time. Of course, I realize my mistake
now, fully. That's why I'm working like this, day and
night, filling reams of paper, using gallons of ink, neglect-
ing all the ordinary part of life which has, for me, become
supremely unimportant.

He looked out of the window with a vacant smile. Snow
was floating in the air, alighting on the massed umbrellas
and there dissolving. The people underneath were but-
toned into dark coats, he noted, wore stout boots that made
their feet seem large and clumsy as they struck the pavement. A thin black mud covered the ground. It would be
dusk early today. The clouds swam low and heavy over the
roofs. To imagine oneself above them, in an aeroplane,
flying through limitless sunshine at the speed of sound,
produced a sense of intoxication, like that experienced
during some confused, extravagant dream.

'I believe it is a dream,' he murmured. 'That's why I
keep hearing the doors quietly opening and shutting all
over the house.' He listened and, sure enough, there it was
again: click, click, soft bang, slight rattle of a handle.
These sounds were audible only to the keenest attention,
and the smallest movement, such as crossing the legs, or

taking a handkerchief from a pocket, drowned them. Sometimes he went on to the landing, or down into the hall, and observed the doors narrowly. They never moved while he watched. He would try to remember whether they were in the same position as on his last inspection. But, though it often seemed that a proportion of them were, he never felt certain which ones, or even, on second thoughts, that any remained stationary.

In an effort to be scientific and methodical, he had shut them all one morning. Later in the day, however, he had occasion to enter several of the rooms and, being pre-occupied with problems of different sorts, might not have closed them behind him, as he had fully intended to do. Sometimes his thoughts were so voluminous that actions such as going to the bathroom, or taking in the milk were entirely automatic and left no more trace on his memory than if he had walked in his sleep. How was it possible, under these circumstances, to recollect the exact positions of half a dozen doors?

Yet the matter was supremely important and had a bearing not only on the state of his ears, click-click, but also on the flickerings in the mirror. He rarely looked up now without seeming to see reflected in it the end of a movement in the room behind him; a swirl in the air as if someone had just left; or poked a head round the door and taken it back instantly; or the suggestion of a shadow, sinking out of sight before the eye could focus. These phenomena worried him because he had not sufficient leisure to devote to their elucidation. Naturally, they had their own laws and motivations which could be discovered by the patient experimenter, but it was impossible for the human mind to concentrate on two things at once.

'If the truth of all those days and you and me and Mrs

Strumbold is to be nailed,' he muttered, striking his fist on the arm of the sofa, 'then many other interesting aspects of experience will have to be neglected. How it snows. It's quite a blizzard.'

He saw a man balancing a box on top of the gate while he fiddled with the catch, his fingers cold and clumsy. But there was no need to do anything because he had given orders over the telephone that the groceries were to be left in the front porch and the bell rung twice as a signal. So he watched Toby clumping across the bottom half of the mirror. Only his head and part of the box were shown. He saw him look up inquisitively at all the windows.

After two sharp rings, there was a pause as Toby listened carefully and squinted through the letter-box. But he could see only a small strip of hall and three bottom stairs. Why, the old looney might have fallen down dead and no one would know, he thought greedily, his mind full of telly dramas and accumulated titbits from the newspapers. Only last week there'd been a story of a miser who'd knocked hisself silly in a cupboard under the stairs and not been found for a fortnight. It was well known that old Platt had a tidy bit stored away somewhere. How else could he have afforded all them orgies? Nothink was so expensive as women, especially the ones that went in for anythink peculiar. His eyes bulged through the letter-box.

The house within remained perfectly silent. Joseph sat motionless in front of the glass, waiting to see the man off. The sound of the groceries being put on the step, and of the letter-box being opened, had come clearly up to him. There had been no ambiguity about these noises. It was possible to place them at once and to deduce their source without the smallest doubt. He felt that this threw further

85

light on the business of the doors, opening and shutting like a heartbeat all day long. He was now certain that they did and that heads were put round them and piercing stares directed at his shoulders bent over the page as the pen flew left, right, left, right and used sheets accumulated on the table, sofa, floor, bed, mantelpiece and other handy surfaces.

Toby had difficulty in withdrawing his eyes from the letter-box. The black silence fascinated him. He was sure the place was full of people. It had that feeling. They must be standing behind the half-open door he could see through the front window; or lined up in those parts of the hall invisible from his peephole; or leaning over the up-stairs banisters naked. A delightful shiver passed over him and he did not know how to get himself down the path and back into his delivery van. But he must. His boss was strict and knew exactly how long a round should take.

Joseph watched his departure into the snow. It was now lying thinly here and there on the roofs. The flakes were getting larger, tumbling quickly down the sky like an in-vasion. They were blotting out the view. The people in the road had become shadows, faint indications of human-ity; or perhaps they were only memories of persons once encountered under other circumstances and in a different place. It was hard to make any plain statement of fact, Joseph thought, when everything was swirling in front of one's eyes like a kaleidoscope. When there was so much movement inside and outside the house. When one could not be sure whether one's own personality were dissolving into a new pattern. Or just dissolving.

Suddenly he felt the need to speak to someone. The delivery man had gone and was, in any case, not suitable. He might rush out and halt the shadows under the umbrellas, saying, 'It's not my wish to be a hermit, but I have important tasks to perform, requiring all my energy. How do I know if there is time to spare for amusements? Don't think I'm a killjoy. It is far from the case. I believe fervently in relaxation and fun of all sorts. The world would be less dangerous if human beings were more frivolous. If they were devoted to trivial ends which never roused the passions. Thus, wars, politics, religion, big business and every kind of jealousy would become things of the past and paradise would settle down on earth for ever. But this is an impossible dream, I know. It is one of many I have had here, in that room of which you can just glimpse the window behind the storm. Friends and neighbours! You cannot imagine how I long to enjoy your freedom; to walk up and down, up and down, with an umbrella safely over my head and my mind at rest. For the life of a hermit is immensely strenuous.'

As he spoke, the ghosts would gather round him, staring and muttering in the darkness under their umbrellas. They would, perhaps, form a complete circle so that he would be unable to regain the house and would be swallowed up and forced to go along with them to their destination. Instead of taking this sensible course, which would have extricated him at one blow, he stopped short just inside the front door at the telephone and dialled the number of one of his most fervent readers.

He could hear it ringing and ringing in her empty flat. She was evidently out gossiping elsewhere. So he consulted the worn bit of paper with the numbers kept for these emergencies.

'Hello.'

'Hello. Joseph here.'

'Joseph! How lovely....'

'Listen, I've a message. It's important. Have you a

pencil? Good. I may not be able to speak to you again on account of certain barriers behind which I have somehow become entrenched. What I mean is—'

'But are you the *right* Joseph?'

'Don't interrupt. Time is horribly short. I wish to record a statement to the effect that I never intended any harm to anyone, much less my dearest Nancy, whose happiness was always my first concern. Whatever occurred was against my express wishes. I hope to make that plain in the later chapters of my narrative. But who knows whether I shall ever reach them? I have had presentiments and there are bad omens as well. The doors keep opening and I can't get the manuscripts back into the cupboards. They simply won't fit any more. Is it right, is it reasonable that I should be persecuted in this manner?'

'I'm afraid I can't help you. It must be the wrong number.'

'Hold on, for God's sake, even if it is the wrong number, which I don't believe for an instant. You're just being difficult. I've caught you in an unsympathetic mood, worse luck. Have a little patience. You won't regret it. And stop using that assumed voice. Such an affected accent. Sorry, I didn't mean to offend you! I hardly know what I'm saying. It's the effect of overwork and the strain of deciding on what is the truth. For there wouldn't be this great drift of manuscripts in all the rooms, without exception, if I could distinguish the truth beneath the many suppositions with which it has become encrusted during my struggles. Why don't we have dinner together and then I can explain properly and you can give me your advice? It's a philosophical problem, really, and it may be that your study of Berkeley would come in useful. I ought to have read his works myself, I know, but days pass, years pass, decades even, and one hasn't accomplished a quarter of the programme laid out in optimistic moments when time and strength seemed limitless.'

At this point he became aware that the woman, whoever she was, had hung up. In a way, he was glad since it meant that he would have to go back to his work. 'Back to you, darling. Back to real life.' All the doors seemed to have taken up new positions.

12

WE sat at the kitchen table, speaking in low voices so that Mrs Strumbold should not hear us from the sitting-room where she had been settled with a pornographic book. I had been obliged to become a frequenter of certain shops, otherwise we should never have had a moment to ourselves. 'At my age, you have to enjoy life by proxy,' said the old woman with a scowl. 'And why shouldn't I? I know what I like. Get me something with a bite in it, for God's sake. No more of this kids' stuff.' I had tried my best.

'Don't be disappointed, darling,' I said in a rapid monotone. 'One's hopes are always slightly dashed. My novel hasn't come up to expectation, let's face it. But that's nothing unusual in an author's world. It's one of those natural phenomena for which one should make allowance in any plan of action. I mean, it's a sensible thing to map out the future, but one doesn't want to be too rigid. One must be ready to take advantage of circumstances as they actually present themselves. Don't be disheartened,' I cried ardently, putting your hand inside my coat to try to warm it. 'Literature is full of ups and downs. That's its charm. I knew a writer once who had the most terrible struggles. He tried funny stuff, murder, politics, famines, mountaineering, exploration, science fiction. Nothing went more than so-so, and he didn't know who to borrow from in order to head off the worst of his creditors. Most of his friends were like me, munching raw cabbage in an insalubrious basement.'

'That might be better than this,' you sighed. Your hand was like a stone against me.

'Oh, I don't think so!' I exclaimed in horror. 'I must differ from you there. I speak as an experienced pauper. But to return. After many years of terrible luck my friend hit on the solution: books by black men always sold. So he made an arrangement with a nigger of his acquaintance. This fellow stood in for him at all public appearances and his photograph was put in the advertisements. My friend began a series of violent novels, full of sainted blacks and villainous whites. They were set in South Africa, the southern states of America, Kenya, Rhodesia, the Congo. Neither of them had ever been to these places, because they'd never been able to afford the fare to anywhere further from London than Brighton, and that only at rare intervals. But now everything changed,' I cried, quite carried away by my vision of prosperity, getting up and standing on the table, as if addressing a multitude. You gazed at me, hunched in your chair. Your mouth was wide open.

'These books were translated into every European language. The Americans lapped them up. There were films, plays, telly appearances. Lectures had to be refused. The dark stand-in couldn't manage them, even if the whole thing was written out. He had difficulty with his reading. In spite of his limitations, he had quite a success at short interviews as his inability to utter anything other than swear words was put down to shyness. Also, he was photogenic, having a receding forehead, huge eyes, pronounced jaw and general air of starvation — in the beginning, that was.'

'Why, this is only kids' stuff after all,' yelled Mrs Strumbold from the sitting-room. 'How can an old person like me get a thrill out of such innocence? It's vapid.'

'Persevere, madam,' I shouted back immediately. 'I believe you will find the next chapter much more interesting. That book is intended to have a cumulative effect.'

'It had better,' she growled.

I jumped off the table and took you in my arms: 'Don't worry, sweetheart, it distresses me so. I only tell you my little fable in order to demonstrate how luck changes in an instant, perhaps when one is least expecting it. My friend became immensely famous and affected not to know me when I waylaid him in the street one day, with a manuscript in my hand. Then his black *alter ego* was run over. But we needn't continue the story, darling. One stage at a time is enough. It's a great mistake to anticipate trouble.'

'I've had the sack,' you sobbed.

'What?' I cried, letting go of you. 'Say that again.'

'Sack,' you said. 'Buzzed out with a week's pay.' Your face was quite grey with fear.

'How can that be so?' I muttered, pacing round the table at speed. 'The food, the gas, the light, hot water, coal, soap, rates, etc., depend on your wages for the time being. True, it's not a very dignified position for a man to be in, but I bear it in the interests of literature and the future. Hah! Do you mean to tell me that these excellent arrangements have crashed through your negligence?'

'I don't know how it happened,' you wept.

'Heh, heh, heh,' laughed Mrs Strumbold in a paroxysm. 'This is an improvement, I must admit.'

'I realize that bossess of yours is temperamental.' I rejoined in a reasonable voice, 'but there must have been some previous indications, surely? She cannot simply have handed you your money without a word of explanation?'

'I typed everything wrong,' you wailed.

'But why did you?' I asked, trying my best to put on a kind and reassuring manner. 'Has anything upset you lately? I thought we were progressing particularly well. It's true that one of the exciting things about our situation is that I don't understand you in the least. I never have an idea of what's passing in your mind. Every night is a new adventure. Marvellous! Yet, there are disadvantages. Please explain the circumstances of your dismissal. I can't advise you unless I have all the facts.'

'She said if I mucked up one more letter, it'd be the end,' you replied sullenly.

'Then why did you?' I enquired, much struck by a sudden flash of Mrs Strumbold in your face.

'How do I know?' you shrieked. 'Because I did!'

'Yes, but darling, consider,' I rejoined in a propitiating voice. 'The consequences of such rashness are not disposed of so easily. The Nook and all its contents are at stake. Our future is cast into the melting pot. For if I am again prevented from pursuing my career through adversity, it may be the *coup de grâce* as far as I'm concerned. An artist's faculties are very precariously balanced and, once interfered with, difficult to re-establish in proper working order. It is necessary to be free from worries of all sorts and to live as quietly and uneventfully as possible if the maximum concentration of mind is to be attained, as it must be for the production of true art. You see how disastrous it would be if our little society in The Nook were broken up. It would be the end of me, as I say, but that's not the most important aspect. I'm ready to believe that I overestimate my own worth. No, it's of you and Grandma that I chiefly think. I can't bear the idea of you both coming to grief for lack of a little forethought, a little self-discipline, Nancy, and attention to business.'

'I didn't mean to type it wrong,' you remarked, evidently bored by my well-meant homily. 'My fingers just wrote of their own accord.' You handed me a bit of paper from your bag.

There was a large footprint in the middle and a certain amount of lipstick in one corner. In spite of this, I clearly read: 'Dear Sir, Further to your esteemed order of the 18th instant, I think you are plain horrible and how you can pretend to enjoy it is beyond me.'

'Why,' shouted Mrs Strumbold in a great rage, 'the illustrations are the same as in the last book I had. It's a swindle!'

I took no notice of the interruption, except to lower my voice still further beneath the murmuring tones I had employed thus far: 'What's the meaning of this? Are you mad? Besides, it's the opposite of what you said at the time.'

With an ambiguous smile, you gave me another letter which showed signs of having been screwed up and carefully flattened after rescue from a wastepaper basket. It was addressed to a manufacturer in Hull: 'Dear Sir, An extensive search has been made for the information you require and I think you must be a feeble performer, or something. Otherwise surely it would be more like what it says in the books.'

I was dumbfounded. It was such a travesty of everything that had happened between us. As for typing it into the office letters, I would never have suspected you of so much originality. I looked at you with new admiration. 'Sweetest,' I ventured humbly, 'may I suggest that this tone of criticism is hardly the right treatment for the amelioration of the condition you describe so succinctly. Not that I'm prepared to admit that there's a word of truth in what you say. But I'm ready to humour your fancy and to make allowances for ignorance and weak nerves. It's all due to lack of reading on your part. Why Grandma should have brought you up in such simplicity, I cannot imagine.'

I drew you on to my knee and kissed your neck, just to show that I spoke only for your own good and quite without hard feeling. I never experienced the least approach to hard feeling for you, even at the worst. I'm ready to swear to it on oath, if required. As these protestations passed swiftly through my head, you were fishing in your bag which seemed to be full of odd bits of paper. 'Heavens above.' I said, 'why didn't you tell me about this? We could have had a few chats and cleared the whole thing up in a jiffy. You had no need to go to such lengths in order to attract my attention. Besides, what good has it done? You've got yourself the sack just at the very moment when we owe all round because I had to spend some money on a decent suit. I have to be prepared for public appearances. Suppose someone rich should invite me to lunch, or to stay at his country mansion? I might be asked to lecture, or to declare something open. You know every one of my trousers was patched in the seat, because you mended them yourself, very neatly, too; don't think I'm ungrateful. But the fawn pair, you remember, were done with a strip off the dark-brown curtains and the black ones with a clean corner of that chair cover Grandma ruined with knitting-needles, cough mixture, raspberry juice and boot blacking. I only mention these matters in order to remind you of the essential part you have in my life.'

While I spoke, in soothing tones, for I knew you were upset, you spread the papers edge to edge on the table like a cloth. The unshaded light glared on them and cast our double shadow sharply over the sink. We both leaned forward and eagerly read the legends: 'He does it from spite. I shall stab him one day. I will poison his food. What about false charges? Isn't he carrying on with Grandma? I hate

95

him, hate him, hate him. I'll hang myself like I saw in that film. I can't do without him. Suppose I should have a baby? Oh, God, don't let that happen.'

'There is no need to address the deity on that score,' I remarked. 'A family doesn't figure in my plans at all.'

You pointed to a letter in the centre of the table. It was dated that very day and said, in block capitals: 'Dear Sir, We regret that we cannot supply you with the goods listed in yours of the 30th ult. He sleeps so heavily afterwards. It'd be easy to light a fire. We'd be better dead.'

'I believe if we collaborated over a book, it would be a roaring success,' I cried enthusiastically. 'You have such an original imagination. That bossess ought to have promoted you. You're worth your weight in gold. We'll make a fortune. You'll see.' I covered every available part of you with kisses which you reciprocated in a manner that made me forget the near presence of Mrs Strumbold.

'Heh, heh, heh,' her laughter filled the house. 'It must be fifty years since I tried this one. How time passes when you're not looking. At my age, one lives in one's memories too much.'

'Let's make certain we have entertaining memories,' I whispered. 'We don't want to get melancholy in the years to come. So many people go into a decline from sheer boredom. It's an end to be avoided at all costs. That's one of the reasons why writing is important. It keeps the faculties brisk. And don't forget, darling, that there's a lot in it for you. I have had some very encouraging reviews. You can't deny it. You've read them yourself. It's true they've been rather few and far between but one can't leap to the head of one's profession all in a moment. I assure you it's impossible. Ascents are inevitably gradual. My next book which is another variation on you, me and Grandma, will bring me definitely to the fore. I could relate several anecdotes concerning well-known people to prove my point, but I don't wish to seem vain, even with you, before whom I am least ashamed of anyone in the world.'

I spoke in a passion and gripped you round the waist and neck. With a short titter, you turned your bag upside down in the middle of the table. A heap of paper fell out, accompanied by lipstick, powder, combs, brushes for the eyelashes, bus tickets, string, pencils, money. You put the empty bag on my head, like a hat. The opening was just large enough and the handle hung down over my left ear. I was glad to see you in such good spirits and though it seemed to me a poor joke, on the whole, I smiled encouragingly.

'You see, darling,' I continued, stroking your back, 'how I depend on you for everything. That glorious, rich future will be for ever a mirage if you allow yourself to type this kind of letter during office hours. They are wonderful creations. I could scarcely do better myself. But there are times when it's necessary to curb the imagination in the interests of survival. You won't have any difficulty in getting another job, sweetest, because you're so efficient, so honest, so good, and I love you much too much to let you fall by the wayside. We'll go to the agency first thing tomorrow and get you fixed up. Fortunately I reached the end of a chapter this morning and can be conveniently interrupted for a day or two until things are settled. For I don't want to rush you into some firm where, perhaps, you would not be happy. What an idea! You must feel quite free to reject the first offer if it doesn't seem suitable. If you think the boss might make objectionable advances, for instance; or the employees appear vulgar, or foul-mouthed.' I adjusted the bag on my head.

'But I didn't write these letters,' you said. 'They just

happened by themselves. I was so surprised when I read them.'

'How is that possible without the help of ghosts?' I argued earnestly. 'The machine must be struck by intelligent hands if words are to be formed, let alone coherent sentences. Besides, darling, you must admit that though these are not your real sentiments, yet they reflect thoughts which have passed through your mind at overwrought moments.'

'They are my real thoughts,' you said stiffly. 'Why are you wearing my bag in that stupid way?'

I took it off with great relief as the metal part was pressing on my temples and making it hard to concentrate. 'That is just what I said,' I cried triumphantly. 'There is no disagreement between us at all. A little care, a little self-discipline, and you will soon be out of this slough of despond. I've experienced similar moods myself and I know that they pass. But I do think it's necessary for you to realize that these letters could not exist unless you had typed them. Would the bossess have been so cruel as to give you the sack if there could be any doubt in the matter; if it was conceivable that they were the work of nimble-fingered spirits?'

'I'm sick of reading,' shouted Mrs Strumbold. 'Where's my Ovaltine?' There was a bang as though a book had violently hit the skirting-board.

'Patience, madam, I'm putting on the milk,' I called.

'I wasn't one of her favourites,' you said, gathering the letters into a pile. 'She wanted an excuse to get rid of me. A girl with red hair had come asking for a job and she couldn't be taken on unless somebody went. She collected girls with red hair. There were two already.'

'Oh, in that case, I don't wonder she seized on the opportunity,' I said musingly, for this threw a new and alarming light on the bossess. 'You haven't even any coppery tints. But apart from that, which could be remedied quite simply with a bottle from the chemist round the corner, there was the matter of the letters to the merchant of Hull, and others. Here, I think, she had reason for annoyance. It must have caused delay in the correspondence and time is money in business. Competition is cut-throat and the fastest turn-round wins the day.'

How I wished I were a psychiatrist, darling, the right phrases flickering on the end of my tongue of themselves. For it was plain to me that you had some desperate sort of complex which, if not promptly cured, would be the cause of endless complications in our life. I longed so much for everything to go calmly and without effort on my part. I was sure it was the happier course, though, naturally, anything concerning yourself was of immense interest to me, and indeed, inspiring in a way I had never experienced in my various adventures since leaving the parental village in Yorkshire.

'We will never go to Yorkshire, anyway,' I said aloud. 'Anything would be better than that.'

Before I could protest, you had struck a match and lit the pile of paper on the table. The flames would have singed you, had I not snatched you back. 'What next?' I exclaimed angrily. 'I intended to file those letters with my notes. Careless girl. Who knows what use I might have made of them in time to come, if not immediately? What stories, essays, and learned dissertations on the fate of humankind I might not have extracted from them?'

'Oh, but the flames are lovely,' you said. 'I like the smell of the smoke, too.'

'Don't breathe it up so deeply,' I said, alarmed. 'You will suffer from disagreeable after-effects. I really think we ought to pour a jug of water over them before they set the curtains on fire. Besides, the table must be getting badly scorched. Nothing gives such an impression of poverty and failure in a home as half-burnt furniture.'

'Tee-hee,' you tittered.

'It's no laughing matter,' I returned severely. 'People judge by appearances to an astonishing degree. They draw adverse conclusions from blackened ceilings and sooty walls. If it was well known that we were rich and successful, it would be put down to eccentricity. As things are, the worst construction will be placed on it,' I sighed, wishing you had slightly more intellect and could take my meaning without needing so many explanations. I listened intently, but there was no sound from the sitting-room. Mrs Strumbold must have fallen into a sudden sleep, as often happens with old people.

You yawned prodigiously and reached for the matches.

'Darling,' I said persuasively, 'I must protest against these pyrotechnics, even though they indicate the sort of original approach to things that I admire. Please believe that. But circumstances dictate caution. I'm still in debt. You have been sacked. Grandma hasn't enough money for three. It requires very little head for business to draw the correct conclusions from these premises. It is not even necessary to go to the trouble and expense of pencil and paper. One can do it on one's fingers.'

You looked at me through your fingers, saying, 'Why not grow a beard?'

'Too inflammable,' I said, dismissing the subject at once, for I didn't wish to be distracted from the main stream of my thought. I always had difficulty in collecting myself once that happened. For one thing led imperceptibly to another and, in no time at all, I was gyrating in a superb new dimension, full of ideas quite different from those experienced hitherto, which, in retrospect, seemed as though they must have belonged to somebody else. It was a delightful sensation, but not conducive to the solution of urgent problems.

So I continued firmly: 'The question of beards is not one which can be settled off-hand. I'm not against them in principle. It's simply that the present is not a propitious moment for decisions of that sort. For the fact is that you're tired, darling, and no wonder after the ups and downs you've had today with that ungrateful bossess. Who, in her senses, would not be flattered, honoured, exalted, by having such a one as you at her beck and call? No matter. A good night's sleep is what you need in order to face to-morrow's tasks.' I stroked you as I spoke, hoping to quiet your nerves sufficiently to enable me to let go of you and reach the jug of water on the draining-board behind us. The table was definitely smouldering.

'A rest, a rest, a good deep sleep,' I intoned in what I hoped was a hypnotic voice. 'Don't worry. Women have strange turns. I once started to read a huge work in eight volumes on the subject, but had not the stamina to finish it. How I wish I had been more industrious. It would have saved me much subsequent perplexity. I believe you're beginning to feel very sleepy. I'll take you upstairs.'

You had put your arms round my neck and your head on my shoulder. A small patch on the table glowed red in the draught from the door. All at once, you bit me under the ear.

What sharp teeth! I could not repress a cry. We struggled. The chair and table overturned. We fell on the floor. I was frightfully angry. Months of restraint and consideration for your feelings had resulted only in this contemptuous gesture. For your face, though terrified, was full of contempt as you lay on the ground, half choked with my hands on your throat and my blood dripping into your mouth. I had taken the trouble to cultivate a sensitive awareness of your needs, despite the fact that such an approach was clean against the grain of my own character. Forgetting that you were a Strumbold too, I had thought to save you from Grandma's tyranny, her bestiality, her cannibalism. But now I realized in a frenzy that I had been taken in, taken over, made use of and out-manœuvred by a couple of Strumbolds masquerading as helpless females, ready prey for a prowler of unscrupulous ambition.

'Do you imagine any man of spirit is going to stand such treatment?' I yelled, although my lips were at the most two inches from your own. 'I'm not, I can assure you here and now. I took up residence in this house on certain assumptions which we needn't go into at the moment. Arrangements of a definite sort were made and a *quid pro quo* agreed on. Please remember that. I'm the boss of The Nook and, what's more, I'm an artist and it would be entirely wrong for me to toil in some dead-end job while you and Grandma graciously allowed me to pay the bills and watch you getting madder every day. I have no intention of allowing that to happen. You have been offered the chance of nurturing a genius and I insist on your taking it.'

'Sacked,' you articulated, as well as you could. 'Be sacked again by next firm. Can't help typing wrong letters. Your fault.'

'How can it be my fault?' I expostulated violently. 'I never advised anything of the kind. It is quite contrary not only to my wishes, but also to my knowledge of the business world. I've been on the staff of newspapers and I know how tricky the position of employee is. Why, even with the most benevolent boss, one can't be too careful. Suddenly the accountant says the yearly balance isn't correct and three people will have to be disposed of before December the 31st. So you see, darling,' I ended on a pleading note, 'you must pull yourself together. Literature depends on your taking a sensible view. If I don't follow up my present book with another as quickly as possible, I'll never make it. There are nights when I have bad dreams.'

'So do I,' you said, gloomily. My hands had relaxed, enabling you to speak fairly easily. Smoke was getting rather thick in the room, curling up from the table as it lay on its side. The blood had almost completely dried on us. I settled myself more comfortably against you. We leant our heads together on the cupboard under the sink.

'Ah, dreams,' I said tenderly. 'Why let them disturb you? They're due to some quite simple extraneous cause, such as eating too much, or being over-tired so that your nerves are on edge before you sleep. I recommend reading something dull, flat and platitudinous when you get into bed. I have found sermons answer the purpose very well. Evangelical Victorians for preference. There is such a feeling of damp irrelevance in their repetitious paragraphs; they summon up so keen a picture of gaunt pseudo-Gothic interiors filled to capacity with nodding congregations, that one slips off smoothly, without realizing it, darling, one's mind untroubled. Those worthy divines have a profoundly important place in the history of humankind. They have brought sleep to thousands of tired souls who, on waking, were better able to deal with the problems that oppressed them. Let me lend you volume thirteen of my collection. It's far the best for our purpose. I bought the lot for ten shillings at a time when I was flush and I've never regretted it. In the morning, sweetheart, everything will seem different, I promise you. We'll go to the agency together and I shall see to it personally that you are fixed up with a decent boss, or bossess, as the case may be.'

I kissed you again and again as we lay on the floor among

103

the crumbs of our supper. Perhaps the smoke intoxicated me. The heat was also considerable by now. These factors combined with the Protestant omnipotence expressed by the sermons we had been discussing, induced in me a strong feeling of optimism and a certainty that, in the end, everything would turn out as I most desired.

'Heh, heh, wah, ug, hug,' spluttered Mrs Strumbold, whose existence I had, for the moment, entirely forgotten. 'This is a new variation, I see. Have to burn the house down before you can get any satisfaction. Have to roast your Grandma in order to enjoy life. Wa-ug, blug.'

She hobbled rapidly from the tap to the table with jugs of water in each hand, muttering meanwhile in a choked monotone: 'Dare say it's explained in one of those stodgy books you bought me, but they've no proper index. What's the use of a book on a serious subject without an index? And the captions to the pictures are so stupid. And the descriptions have no bite at all. You don't try, you good-for-nothing boyfriend you. Anything'll do for an old idiot like me. What makes you think I'm in my dotage?'

Here we received most of a jugful as her hand shook with rage. The room was full of sizzling and a smell of wet ash. The old woman's shadow swooped across the walls, now behind her, now in front as she passed backwards and forwards under the light. The smoke lay heavily under the ceiling and magnified her voice:

'They think they can suffocate me, just for their amusement. What a mistake. That's not the basis on which they have free board and lodging at The Nook. What gave you such silly notions?' She kicked me with a sharply pointed shoe.

'I never had them,' I returned sullenly. 'Haven't I worked harder for your comfort than anyone? Haven't I laboured? Haven't I slaved? As cook, housekeeper, daily woman, gardener and librarian? What limit have you put to my duties?'

'None whatever,' said she with surprise. 'Why should I? You said you didn't mind what you did as long as there was time for your writing.'

'There's just time, if I hurry,' I admitted.

'Well then,' said Mrs Strumbold, contemptuously emptying another jug over me, 'what are you complaining of? Why shouldn't you hurry? Is it my fault that the reception of your novel has only been so-so?'

'Many people have disappointments,' you put in drowsily.

'Oh, I'm not blaming you for the reviews, or for the sales,' I said to Mrs Strumbold. 'But I do think that if you had a little more patience with the problems of an artistic temperament we would not have reached the impasse where we are now stuck. Also, I should like to state categorically that it's not due to my negligence that the level of pornographic literature has fallen far below the exciting standards you remember from your youth.'

'Bah,' said Mrs Strumbold. 'What do you know about it?'

'Bloody know-all,' you murmured.

'Hush, darling,' I remonstrated, clasping you tenderly as we lay in the water, two inches deep thanks to Grandma's amazing agility 'This is not the right moment for you to intervene. You will only upset yourself. Let me deal with Grandma on your behalf. I am a man of wide reading, though it's true I haven't found her case exactly described. Never mind! I shall do it myself and then you will be able to retire, sweetheart. It is my ambition that you should live in utter sloth and laziness, since that's what you really desire. It's simply the necessity of money which makes us put off the millennium with a visit to the employment agency.'

'You've said it,' remarked Mrs Strumbold, patting her hair with sudden coquetry.

'Madam!' I exclaimed, incensed beyond bearing. 'Who is going to mop up all this water I should like to know? It is just slopping over the door sill and has, I suppose, seeped into a good part of the hall and the sitting-room, too, most likely. You have flooded the place out of spite. It won't look the same again, no matter how much scrubbing and wiping is done. You should consider before turning on taps in that reckless manner. You have probably reduced the value of The Nook by several hundred pounds.'

Though entirely reasonable in the circumstances, my remonstrance seemed to induce great hilarity in Mrs Strumbold, who took unnecessary risks with her health, I thought, standing in water at her age. 'Heh-heh,' she spluttered. 'Too much water! That's what's wrong. It's wonderful to be so educated. You put your finger on the vital point immediately. Clever boyfriend. I congratulate you, Nancy. Didn't I always say you'd never regret his proposals?'

'Haven't,' you mumbled from a dream. I squeezed you thankfully.

Mrs Strumbold fished in her bosom and produced a key, attached to her neck by a string on which were also, I now perceived, lucky charms, lockets and a small purse. She approached a cupboard I had never previously seen unlocked. 'Too much water,' she repeated. 'We'll soon put that right, you prosy little boyfriend.'

I tried to assume a dignified air, feeling that more honour than this was surely due to a budding author, some of whose reviews had been distinctly better than so-so. My teeth chattered with cold and damp as I tried to formulate an appropriate response. But I was terrified in case the cupboard should prove another unsuspected lair of obscenities: horrible wigs, bangles, dresses, button boots, parasols, all of a size easily worn by a smallish man, like myself. I cannot describe my relief on seeing that it contained only six empty whiskey bottles.

Mrs Strumbold, however, was adversely affected. 'You slut,' she screamed. 'You've picked the lock. You've drunk it secretly. Your mother was just the same. A thieving little rat as soon as my back was turned.'

'Oh, dearest,' I could not avoid saying, 'why did you never tell me of this cache? It would have helped so much in those middle chapters where I got into difficulties.'

I was extremely surprised when the old woman snatched a bottle and broke it over your head. What savagery! Worse still, she took hold of a splinter and advanced on your prostrate form. Luckily, I had sufficient presence of mind to jump up and catch her arm. The most extraordinary reflections and shadows rippled across the ceiling as we swayed together in front of the cupboard.

13

Joseph paused and licked his lips. He felt hungry for some reason, although it was not long since he had eaten. He did not think so, at least. But it was possible that more time had passed than he realized. The clock had stopped. He ought really to have an electric one, revolving silently and endlessly as his life slipped away in this room. Was it even the same day as during his last fit of consciousness when, as he clearly remembered, he had opened a tin of soup and one of chicken and boiled them up together? He got up, yawned, stretched and looked sharply into the mirror. The door was slightly open. Yet, he had shut it very firmly he knew, on account of icy draughts round the feet which much reduced his powers of concentration.

On examining the door itself, however, he discovered that it was now latched The noise of his turning from the mantelpiece would have drowned the extremely soft click of its closing. For these ghosts were marvellously light-fingered. They could rustle through the papers in the cupboards without displacing one of them. It would be possible to write a most interesting treatise on the nature and habits of ghosts from recent experience and also on the problem of how best to live in their company. For once they had taken over your house, there didn't seem to be any certain way of getting rid of them. Why hadn't powders and gases been invented, similar to those used against cockroaches and rabbits? In this modern age, one ought to be able to rid oneself of all vermin simply by ordering the right tin of poison from the grocer.

One should be able to lift the receiver and say: 'Send me seven pounds of Gosto and charge it to my account, which is, I believe, fully paid up to date.' Then Toby the vanman would come staggering inquisitively along the path and there would be a louder bang than usual as he dropped the box on the steps, never worrying whether it contained eggs or other fragile goods. When Toby had finally gone, he would creep downstairs, open the door quickly and drag in the box.

Then he would investigate the Gosto, sniffing it, running it through his fingers, feeling its texture, imagining the ghosts drawing back in horror and making hotfoot for other premises where this preparation was unknown; or the owners did not object to their presence. He would take a spoon, or large sugar sifter, and carefully sprinkle the powder all round the doors and windows, in front of the cupboards, down every crack in the skirting. He would light little piles of newspapers and Gosto in the fireplaces, in order to fumigate the chimneys.

But what about the ones who knocked on the roof and outside walls? Perhaps they would join in the general exodus. He very much hoped so, because it was distracting to have to share the house. Otherwise he would not have minded, or at least would have become sufficiently used to them by this time. The real trouble was that they hadn't grasped the idea of good neighbourliness; of living quietly and unobtrusively in a dark corner; of minding their own business. As a result, he was chapters and chapters behind schedule.

Darling! he thought in the utmost distress How can I speak of you in such terms, even privately and with nobody listening except yourself? What has happened to me that I talk of exterminating you with a form of supernatural insect powder? It is my great happiness that you have condescended to haunt me, watching over my shoulder while I write. Do please believe me. I know it's a rare privilege. It's just that sometimes I'm overcome by weariness and then the idea of Gosto tempts me. It is only one of many devilish modern inventions which have to be resisted if one is to attain peace of mind and also find time to do those things one believes to be important, as much as it's possible to believe anything these days.

He was kneeling on the floor with his chin on the window-sill, staring out on to the snow, which now lay thick and sparkling under a brave sun. It was the sort of weather they were said to have in Switzerland and other favoured resorts: cheerful, invigorating, inconvenient. For many thousands of pipes had frozen, the newspapers said, and a substantial number of elderly people had slipped on the ice, severely damaging their bones. People were skidding and sliding to their deaths in all directions, the reporters further said, except for the large class of aged poor who remained in bed in the hope of keeping warm. What a scandal.

The passers-by seemed comparatively young today. Perhaps it was Saturday or Sunday. They wore red and yellow woollen caps, green coats, blue trousers, white boots and skipped agilely over the lumps of ice with which the pavement was encrusted. Some carried skates. Others dragged toy toboggans, though the nearest hill, Joseph calculated, must be fully two miles off. He had sat with Nancy on the top of it sometimes during August and they had admired the view, especially the enormous gravel pit in the valley, round which a miniture train had pulled endless trucks of sand and stones. But if these people were making for that hill and those pits with their skates and toboggans, they had a goodish walk in front of them. They had not one umbrella among them, in case of a change in the weather, which might easily happen in these notoriously temperamental latitudes. But many had wirelesses screeching in their hands in a distracting manner and others were talking and laughing as if the trees all dressed in frost had made them quite light-hearted.

The Qwikcleen merchant paused at the gate, looked up at Joseph's dead-white face pressed against the window-pane and went on, whistling to himself and at the girls indifferently. He was now stocked up with broad-bladed shovels, stiff brushes and flasks of a certain fluid, which, sprayed over steps, paths, knobs, handrails, windscreens, dissolved the ice like magic and greatly mitigated the dangers of this wonderful continental anticyclone at present enjoyed by a populace far more accustomed to splashing and dripping than to cutting elegant figures of eight on a slippery surface. The only footprints outside The Nook were those of Toby the vanman. It was perfectly useless to waste valuable time and eloquence on one so mad as even to be unable to grasp the self-evident advantages of Warmrap, the cheapest and most effective padded material on the market. Sold by the roll. A thousand uses in the chilly home: round the tank and pipes; down the cracks; between the old folk's blankets, etc. Warmrap saved fuel and enabled the most shrinking to appreciate snow, ice, a bitter north-easter and the prospect of slush to come. Warmrap, warmrap. Sales had been quite encouraging.

'But my good Qwikcleen,' cried Joseph like a drowning man, 'have you no elixir for prisoners such as I? For haunted persons? For men who cannot forget? This house is full of strange miasmas. I have been invaded and that's why I can't escape. I shall never get out alive. I know it.'

The window clouded with his breath, so that he could not see the sparkling scene outside any longer.

'It's not only that my memories have paralysed my will. There's the question of the manuscripts At first, I could just get them back into the cupboards. Next, they overflowed into the rooms. Now there's only enough space left to open the doors and look round them. Everything is buried in paper. Who has written all this stuff? It's beyond the capacity of any single human being. Besides, it doesn't look like my writing. It's too large. It's women's writing. And I can't read what it says, no matter how I try. I can't seem to focus on it, though there's nothing wrong with my eyes in other ways.

'Perhaps if I could open the doors wide enough to reach further into the rooms, I might be able to snatch something legible from underneath. Something to give me a clue, at least. Not a key, no, no, I don't aspire to complete understanding. My apprenticeship, though painful, has not been hard enough for that. No matter how I push, the doors only open sufficiently for me to get one shoulder into the room. That is how it seems, at any rate. It may be that I'm a bit confused here, I've become subject to a curious feeling of bewilderment lately. It's tiring, too. I can hardly keep awake and when I sleep, my dreams are most peculiar.

'Yet that has nothing to do with what I am now trying to say. I only mention these facts about the doors, the writings and the dreams as inexplicable preliminaries to my main statement. I mean, how am I to interpret these manifestations? Sometimes I think the number of presences in the house is increasing at a great rate. The knockings and creakings, the sense of being watched, are almost continuous. Then there is the perpetual rustling and scratching of those who, I suppose, are doing the writing. It would require dozens of pens to cover so much space. I speak as an experienced author.

'But all that is neither here nor there. Why should they not write if they wish? What objection can a reasonable man have to their amusing themselves, day in day out, by opening the doors in order to introduce further manuscripts into the rooms? It's not as if I wanted to use the accommodation for ordinary purposes, such as putting up friends, or lodgers, or tenants of some sort. No, no. I'm all for freedom of choice and non-interference in this world and the next. The sole question is whether their activities are intended for my advancement or not.

'Assuming that they keep on working at the same rate, all the rooms will be full in two months. I don't know how to stop them. Perhaps it's written somewhere Perhaps there's a formula which, once pronounced, would cause the manuscripts to return to their place of origin. But I can't get near enough to search, on account of the doors being supernaturally stiff in the hinges. Even if, by some as yet unknown dispensation, I was able to penetrate, to seize the papers, turn them over and discover the ones appropriate to my work, there's the language difficulty. Or the fact that something happens to my eyes and prevents them from reading. Or it may be that the trouble is due to faulty concentration owing to causes I have not yet been able to disentangle.

'It's not that I mind in the least being an intruder in my own house. I've never been fussy about property, trespassing or fiddling legal questions of any sort. I would be most happy for my darling and her present friends and relations to take over the entire place, except for this room, provided they leave a passage down the stairs and through the hall. How am I to arrange such a compact with them when they can be reached neither over the telephone, nor through the post, nor by any other means I ever heard of?'

There was a sense of laughter behind him, although he could not swear that he had actually heard it. He had a distinct feeling that more papers had suddenly been deposited everywhere. The whole garden was as white as if covered with virgin sheets waiting to be inscribed with complicated secrets which it was essential to unravel if his life were to be preserved. He thought he could just catch the sound of expectant breathing.

'Oh, Qwikcleen,' he shouted in despair and his voice was partly muffled, as if his mouth was full of paper, 'come back and break down the door with your sanity! Throw open the windows and tramp about sneezing with dust and vulgar curiosity. Save me with your incomprehension of everything except of making a profit on a doorstep. Not that I despise the business outlook. Far from it. I beg you to believe me. Hear me. Come with your brushes and shovels. Your dusters and sprays. Your salesman's patter. Trample my dreams and my fantasies under your horrible boots, so that I wake up to freedom. For though the counter-spell is written many times in the manuscripts — indeed I'm certain they contain little else — I shall never find it without you. Qwikcleen; Qwikcleen!' he called, holding out his hands.

14

'B U T darling,' I remonstrated in a startled voice, 'how is it that we are stuck in this extraordinary corner? Why can we not go forward as planned? We had everything most carefully worked out, you remember.'

You said vaguely: 'No, I don't remember '

I took your arm and squeezed it hard, even painfully, so that you would be obliged to give me your attention. 'Do me the honour of listening to what I say,' I cried hotly. 'It's not as if I were speaking of myself. That would naturally be boring. I don't dispute it. I've suffered much from that sort of thing myself. From self-appointed geniuses and other persons similarly inflated.'

'Ha-ha!' you exclaimed, pointing at a photograph of a nude girl in a provocative attitude.

We were walking through the entertainment quarter, as it happened, and the doors between the shops were manned by pimps intoning: 'Non-stop show. Fourteen different girls. Come in and enjoy yourself. Twelve and six. No extras. No catch. They take everything off. Real artists. Enjoy yourself for only twelve and six.'

'It's a swindle,' I remarked gloomily, 'no matter what they say. I went into one of these places just to investigate. It was a question of research. The girls capered in such a cold, perfunctory way, as if they were thinking all the time of a nice cup of tea and putting their feet up. You'd have to be perverted to get a worth-while thrill out of that sort of thing. They don't take the trouble to be provocative, except for the photographer. But can one blame them when it's a non-stop show? Who could keep it up day and night, I ask you?'

'No one,' you said with contempt. 'Typing's the same.'

'How can that be so?' I demanded, trying to keep my voice low and even to prevent the many tourists hovering round the photographs from overhearing. 'It's an honest living, for one thing and, for another, there's a point in it. You're doing it for a real object. What's a passing pleasure compared with happiness which has been worked at for months at a time? You and I are engaged in creating heaven on earth. I feel that most strongly. We must persevere. Faint-heartedness is the worst sin. Lack of energy is fatal. Doubts are poison.'

'Yes, but,' you yawned, 'why must it always be typing? How would you like it?'

'It's a mistake to try to change one's profession after the age of twenty,' I returned, somewhat alarmed by your mood. 'Besides, what else can you do? If you took trouble with your cooking it might be worth something. But it's ten to one you put in sugar instead of salt from sheer carelessness and lack of grip. If I was to write the way you cook the future would be black indeed.'

'Hate cooking,' you said petulantly. 'So much grease and smell.'

'It's because you use too much dripping,' I rejoined warmly. 'And you don't bother to open the window. What can you expect? I'm sure I must have explained this to you a hundred times, but you take no notice for reasons of your own which I'm unable to fathom. That's what makes you so marvellous, darling. I never know what you're thinking. Or if you're thinking at all. A wonderful feeling of uncertainty comes over me as I contemplate your state of mind and I hardly know what I'm doing. Those are the moments when I want to devour you, particularly if you happen to have on that old pink rag of a dress that's tight in the bosom and goes up and down at the hem. It always looks as though it needed a wash,' I continued lyrically, 'even when you've just taken it out of the wardrobe. I've described it exactly in my new book. Oh, sweetheart, you are the heroine of all the books I'll ever write and that's why I have such confidence in them. Why, twenty volumes wouldn't explain the exact significance of you and me and Grandma. On the contrary, they'd be merely a brief introduction. Oh, Nancy, don't let a fatal laziness on your part destroy so remarkable a dream!'

We walked a few yards in silence. I felt rather dizzy. You looked alternately at the nudes and at your reflection in the shop windows. They were small businesses owned mainly by Italians and crammed with sausages, cheese and drink. The Italian girls inside sang love songs which billowed out of the doors and eddied round the pimps, who chanted: 'Foreign films downstairs. The latest from Denmark, Germany, France. English captions. Live show upstairs. The best girls obtainable. Trained dancers. Come and enjoy yourself. No gratuities expected.'

All the houses had signs hanging on them saying, Club. A brisk wind swung these invitations to the gay life. They dipped and sparkled like a flight of birds hovering over the many bits of paper, straw, cardboard and variegated plastic wrappings that bowled along the pavement round our feet. The days were always fine and full of movement, as I remember, darling. People whistled as they went about and young women in high heels and elaborate hair-do's minced continually up and down, like a frieze. There were handcarts selling oranges and handcarts selling eels. The prices were inflated and the goods extremely bad, except for those on the top of the pile. This was supposed to be a wicked quarter and, naturally, huge droves of tourists congregated here, hoping for a refreshing dash of vice.

'But why are we traversing these banal scenes?' I cried, not caring whether anyone stared. 'This commonplace depravity has nothing to do with us. It's so shallow, nothing but idleness and dishonesty of the most conventional kind. If it wasn't that all Grandma's bookshops are in the neighbourhood, I'd never come near it. Let's turn off into some more respectable street, for I've important matters to discuss with you — are you listening now?' I jerked your arm.

'All right, all right,' you said. 'It wasn't my fault the last boss said I wasn't worth my wages.'

'Yes, but,' I protested, 'the last six bosses, and two bossesses as well, have used that identical expression. I must admit with some justification. I find the letters you have typed them amazingly interesting, particularly from the psychological point of view. They're so ingenious, so revealing. In fact, I look forward to reading more of them greatly. But if I were trying to sell soap powder, for instance, or machinery for curling the hair, I believe I would take up a different attitude. I might be angry with you, sweetest, if you can imagine such an event. The idea makes me feel quite shaky, even as a mere supposition, an hypothesis which could be true only if my living depended on the sale of boot stretchers, babies' comforters, or other useful wares. I would never consent to sell rubbish or goods of a purely frivolous kind.'

'I don't believe I shall ever give satisfaction,' you said, leaning against a photograph screwed on to the corner of a building and obscuring the view of several furtive little men.

'Don't give up hope,' I cried. 'Don't fall into despair. It's bad for the nervous system in many ways. Confidence is undermined, often with serious effect on the general mental health. Any psychiatrist will say the same. I've read many of their works and can speak with an authority unusual in a layman. Consider your grandma, how remarkably she keeps going, though now aged ninety-one. I have never read anywhere of anyone remotely approaching her in character, in intellectual power and instinct for self-preservation. That's why I'm convinced my books must be a success in the end. I had dreams of instant notoriety before the first one came out. But I see now that the effect will be cumulative and all the stronger for that.'

'You take a job instead,' you said in a faltering voice. 'You run for the eight o'clock bus every morning, wet or fine. You spend the day copying letters about bubble baths and perfumes and see whether your thoughts get into the typewriter or not.'

'Darling,' I said in the most earnest tones I had yet used, 'you know that would be unwise, not to say impossible. In this hard life we must each of us struggle to the best of our ability to keep our heads above water, to fend the wolf from the door. I am sorry to be sententious. What I mean is that I'm only asking you to keep typing until my books bring in enough for the three of us. I should literally go mad with frustration if I had to break off now and return to the odd-job existence I had before I was so fortunate as to catch sight of you outside those ladies' Turkish baths where we first met.'

'Supposing I should go mad?' you said.

We were now propped against the railings of a square. I gripped the spikes in both hands as I leaned towards you, saying: 'Better you than me.'

'I knew it,' you said with a scream.

I took you in my arms, flattening you against the fence. I cannot describe the feelings that coursed over me as you shook with enormous sobs and struggled to get free. Free! As if anyone could ever attain to that paradise! No wonder your tears poured down my shirt. I stared over your head into the square. Two rows of gigantic plane trees were standing on the grass. Their branches met, making a cool, dark, deserted aisle below. It was strictly private. People like us had to stand without while the cars swished past our legs, spraying us with fumes.

I pulled out my handkerchief and began mopping your beautiful eyes, saying close against your ear: 'Why upset yourself? I didn't mean anything in particular. Besides, what if we should go mad, as you suggest? Would it be so very different from our present state? Only time and experience could tell for certain. But there's no need to take a dim view before it's been proved necessary. Who knows, it might be our salvation. All the problems which oppress us might be solved simply by our not being able to cope with them any more. Stranger things have happened. That's what makes life exciting, whether or not one chances to be incarcerated in The Nook. Oh, what a glorious name that is. So appropriate and so totally mis-leading. Don't wriggle like that, darling. I can hardly hold you.'

I pressed heavily on you in an effort to pin you against the railings. The wind fluttered the tops of the trees inside and many answering shadows slid upon the ground. But in spite of my strength, you broke away and fled along the pavement, your coat flying out behind you like a pair of wings. I gave chase at once, for I was resolved to bring matters to a head between us and to stand no more of those sly evasions at which you were adept. As you wore high heels, I anticipated no difficulty in catching up, though you were light, agile and a good runner. You turned the corner of the square and I saw you through a double set of railings, skimming like a bird.

The traffic obliged you to halt and I seized a strong handful of your coat. 'Stop,' I panted. 'What's the hurry? You cannot suddenly have remembered an important engagement surely, That would be too much of a coincidence. Listen, darling, for God's sake. We can't afford misunderstandings. It's not only a plain question of bills, such as gas, electricity, groceries and warm clothes for the winter. No, no, the real difficulty is that our sojourn on earth is too short. How can we hope to accomplish even half the ambitions, dreams and vague imaginings that daily beset us? One would require to be a god. Or, at least, in touch with one. They have them in Africa, you know,' I whispered soothingly as you trembled in my arms, 'black prophets and prophetesses able to transcend nature, so they say; to live for a hundred years; to visit heaven at will and bring back messages therefrom; to annul the harmful effects of machine-gun bullets by their spells. Oh, sweetheart, what a wonderful country that must be! During my time as a newspaperman, I met a prince of those parts and he told me many marvellous titbits of that sort. He was stabbed by one of his lesser wives shortly afterwards because, in a fit of enthusiasm, he had bought another, inferior, wife a bed with gold knobs.'

At this point, you twisted like a snake and streaked across the road.

'Oh, my darling, what have I said to upset you now?' I cried in horror, rushing in pursuit, not caring who stared or listened to our frantic conversation. 'You are so touchy. It's part of your charm, I admit, but it does also cause complications. How are you able to cover the ground at such a pace, balanced on top of those red heels? It's extraordinary. Nancy, I beg of you, listen to me just once again.'

We were running along a street full of antique shops. Decayed chairs, said to be Chippendale, obstructed the pavement outside some. Others, more expensive, had Victorian desks in the windows with silver candlesticks arranged on them; or stout mahogany tables with coloured wine glasses artfully displayed. There were warming-pans, antlers, pictures of Highland cattle, busts of Socrates, statuettes of horses, plates, vases, footstools worked in cross-stitch.

I had often lingered here, imagining fantastic interiors decorated entirely with these objects and myself standing in front of a large fireplace in a beard, frock coat and striped trousers, one hand on a small round table on which reposed a top hat, a potted palm and a scroll. But now I had not time nor breath for any other thought except the red twinkling of your heels which came and went amongst the crowd.

I caught you by the shoulder and crammed you into a doorway from where a dingy stairs led upwards many flights. Neither of us could speak for a few moments. We were both thankful for this chance to recuperate.

'I don't care what you s-say,' you panted. 'It's all rubbish anyhow.'

'You oughtn't to condemn me before I've said a word in my defence,' I began, trying to keep my voice calm and reasonable since the occasion seemed to demand it. 'Civilization depends on the ability of each and every one of us to uphold the highest principles of conduct, honesty and general fair-mindedness. I have, in my time, written articles to this effect which were well received by editors and public alike, as far as it was possible to tell. For everything is full of imponderables and that's why it's necessary to have plenty of sober discussion before deciding on important changes, new departures, or steps calculated to upset the established equilibrium, whatever that may be,' I ended on a certain note of enquiry, as though there were some doubt about it.

Propped against the dingy wall, you said: 'I'm not going to work for you. I don't believe you're a genius.'

'Come,' I replied in gentle and persuasive tones, 'you mustn't say things you don't mean. My whole way of life depends on my being a genius. I would have been mad to move into The Nook without an ulterior motive.'

'You are mad.'

I took no notice of the interjection because it showed you were in one of your contradictory moods: 'Who would take on your grandma except someone on the lookout for a subject worthy to be enshrined in literature? I may not pay money for the privilege of studying your abominable relative, but surely the cooking, cleaning, insults and special reading should be credited to my account just as if they were golden sovereigns? Have no doubt, darling,' I cried ardently, 'our trials will come to a glorious conclusion. I am certain of it. My instinct for self-preservation and also my artistic sensibilities assure me of it. Besides, I would never impose on a woman's credulity. It would humiliate me too much.'

As I spoke, you gazed at me with an expression for which I was at a loss to account. 'Why,' you now remarked in tones of the greatest amazement, 'you aren't human. You're one of those thinking machines. No wonder I never get any satisfaction.'

'Me cold?' I shouted and my voice rang down the street, halting people in their tracks in the hope and expectation that murder was being done. 'You say that knowing perfectly well my life is centred on you! I've never loved anyone as I do you. Never, never, never. I swear it. You fill my head. I write of no one else, except your grandma. I wait for your return every long hour of the day. Nancy, no one will ever love you as I have done with my whole being, with each breath I take. Everything I do is for you and depends on you. How can you not believe me?'

'I do believe you, but I can't stand it,' you replied, your eyes wide open with terror.

An instant later, you had vanished from the doorway. I renewed the pursuit at once, calling, 'Wait a moment. I can explain. It has to do with the feminine nature which has baffled all writers from antiquity onwards. Let's not give up at this point when we are closer to an understanding than ever before. Besides, we cannot part in any real sense of the term. You know that as well as I. We have been through too much. We are changed from what we were at the beginning of our acquaintanceship. We are no longer free.'

I thought I heard a light voice answer: 'Speak for yourself.' You were by that time out of sight. The next corner had taken you into a street where immense crowds were strolling up and down staring into the shop windows and exclaiming vacantly at waxworks wearing the latest fashions in tweeds, raincoats, cocktail outfits and evening dress. It was impossible to get through them quickly, or to run along the gutter, for traffic was pressed against the kerb in an unbroken line for half a mile at least.

There were many side turnings off that terrible road. I looked into each and could see no sign of you. At certain places, I came to subways and went down them, emerging on the opposite pavement without result. The air was full of sweat, cheap scent, dust and voices talking nonsense

'Oh, my love, what have we done and how has this thing happened?'

I sat down on a doorstep, next to a placard stating: 'Furs. Furs. Furs. For the beautiful woman. For the well-dressed woman. Furs for you. Furs within. Furs.' I had never felt so utterly perplexed in my life.

15

I s that how it really was? Joseph wondered in a nervous frenzy. Did I, for instance, go into that shop and emerge with a small fur collar on approval, having paid a deposit because, as they explained, I was a total stranger to them? Also, the young lady, my fiancée, might damage the collar with lipstick, tea or cigarettes. I don't believe I ever did, he thought, on further reflection. It was only an idea I had after reading the placard. I remember now, I searched my pockets and found only eight and fourpence halfpenny.

He felt triumphant at having settled an important point decisively. It showed he was not going downhill, as an outside observer might have concluded from the immense struggles he underwent in search of those transcendent truths which lay buried in his memory. Was it any wonder that he sometimes got confused? Everyone was liable to get things out of order in moments of tiredness, caused by prolonged concentration. Much encouraged, he stood up and stretched, smiling into the looking-glass where he could see a slight disturbance in the air round the edge of the door.

'There you are, darling,' he murmured, showing his teeth. 'Welcome, welcome. But why do you never come in properly and join me on this sofa? It is of a convenient size for two. It would be much better, as well as less laborious, if you were to tell me the things you want to say, instead of producing those manuscripts which have now silted up the rooms to a height of fully four feet. It's such a waste of time

126

and energy, too — I speak purely from consideration for you — because you use a language I cannot understand. Yesterday, I managed to catch hold of a sheet and drag it out before the door closed on my arm. I couldn't read it, sweetheart, not a word. I don't even know whether it was written in a European language, or something more exotic originating in Africa, or the orient. Or perhaps it wasn't an earthly language. Or it might have been just plain nonsense.'

He paced the hearthrug, weighing up the pros and cons. On the whole, it seemed that there must be some sense in it, simply because it appeared impossible that anyone, ghost or not, would devote so much sustained hard work to the production of utter rubbish. No, he thought, there's certainly a meaning in it. A very important one. But I shall get to the bottom of it, given time. Why should I be afraid that I will not be given time? I'm only middle-aged.

He began counting up the people he had known, or heard or read of, who lived to an enormous age. There must be dozens, for one had to include those whose names were on the tip of one's tongue and couldn't be articulated further. It gave one confidence to do these little sums once in a way. It prevented a feeling of isolation and danger to which he found himself increasingly subject. 'Why should that be,' he enquired in a surprised whisper, 'when I have so much company in the house?'

He had become convinced that a great number of presences had actually settled in. At first, it had seemed probable that they visited in order to deliver and store the manuscripts. This conclusion was based on the fact that the rooms grew more crowded in jerks, instead of filling up continuously, as was now the case. He was resigned to the idea that the lower part of the house would become impassable and that the flood would creep slowly up the stairs towards him. He had therefore written to a marine store and Toby had obligingly posted the letter. Consequently, a rope ladder, neatly rolled, lay under the table beside him. It had hooks which would grip on the window-frame. He had tested them.

Thus, he was able to listen with confidence to the wind in the chimney, which sounded like two people screeching together in the flues, arguing as to the next paragraph, perhaps, or merely exchanging the compliments of the season. It was difficult to decide exactly.

'But all this has nothing to do with it, darling,' he cried, standing on the sofa in order to see farther down the road. The snow was deep over the whole country, the newspapers said. There'd been nothing like it for fifty years. Not only were people skiing, sledging and skating continuously, but also being buried in recurrent blizzards, going into fatal skids and suffering from ruin and starvation owing to the non-delivery of goods. Great banks of black snow had been shovelled into the gutters, much reducing the width of the roadway. Everyone over twenty-five looked pinched and shrunk with the cold, which bit them sharply through the many jerseys and sets of underclothes they wore beneath voluminous coats.

They billow, just as you did while I chased you round the square that day, he thought. The point that worried him was whether he had really caught her up and had a conversation in a doorway. Or whether she had fled straight on and on in front of him until the crowds had hidden her, for ever as it seemed. He was also anxious to make certain that he had not invented the advertisement for furs. It appeared to him that the settlement of this point had far more bearing on subsequent events than he had yet discovered.

Resting one hand on the rope ladder under the table, he

began re-reading the last chapter. He was rather struck by the fact that the writing appeared different from his usual style. There were loops and twiddles and underlinings that gave it a feminine air. He knew that this could not actually be so, chiefly because he was not a woman, or even effeminate. He must either be seeing things, or else the page he held was not part of his projected book at all, but an extraneous manuscript. With a supreme effort of concentration, he focused on the words and read: 'What made you think I was going to put up with your nonsense for ever? Just because you'd made use of me for three years, why did you suppose you could do it for thirty-three? A precious pair, you and Grandma.'

He put down the paper with the utmost amazement, carefully placing half a bottle of glue on the corner to prevent it flying away. 'I don't believe I ever wrote that,' he declared angrily into the looking-glass. 'It doesn't represent my point of view for one thing, and for another, it's a damned lie.'

He took his pen and a clean pad which he examined thoroughly to make sure nothing had previously been written on it. 'I still don't know how we came to such a parting, in the public street, too,' he muttered tremulously, 'but I'm determined to find out. I shall unearth. I shall explain. It's probably quite simple.'

His expression set as he bent over his task. Though the screeching in the flues became louder, he did not hear it; nor the cars and lorries outside the window; nor the people shouting and calling to their friends. For a train had fallen off the embankment into the streets of the town that morning and everyone was excited. A goodish number had been crushed to death and others burnt in a fire started by the upturned engine.

16

I FLUNG open the door saying, 'I've lost Nancy. She ran away. I couldn't catch her. Do you think it would make a difference if I bought her a fur collar? We could put off the coal or the grocer with half-payment.'

'Speak up,' said Mrs Strumbold.

I started again: 'As I was trying to persuade Nancy to apply for a certain job which seemed to me suitable, she took to her heels — those red ones, you know — and I was unable to follow her on account of the huge numbers of persons thereabouts from Birmingham, Manchester, Dublin, Brussels, Paris, Stuttgart, Karachi, Singapore, Yokohama and the Gold Coast.'

'Where were you when this happened?' Mrs Strumbold enquired.

'On the way to your bookshop,' I said, enunciating the words carefully, for the old woman had either grown a little deaf, or else affected this condition for reasons of her own. 'We always visit it on Tuesdays, you remember, because you draw out your old-age pension on Mondays.'

'So I do,' said she in satisfied tones.

'But we never got as far as the bookshop,' I explained defensively, 'on account of the unfortunate accident I have related.'

'Oh, was she run over?' asked Mrs Strumbold in a surprised voice. 'She was always so fussy about looking right and left before putting a foot in the road.'

'No,' I replied, glad to correct her on this point at least. 'In spite of the agitation under which she laboured, she was most careful to observe the traffic regulations as laid down in the various government publications on the subject. In fact, she only crossed the road once and that in perfect safety, owing to nice judgement of speed, distance and converging lines, or points of impact.'

'You mean she suddenly made off when you weren't expecting it?' said Mrs Strumbold, shifting on the chair to ease the rheumatism in her back.

'I had many things on my mind,' I said. 'What to ask for in your bookshop, for example; the title of my new novel; the necessity of persuading her to take the job I mentioned, so that you could go on spending your old-age pension the way you do. Naturally, with all these preoccupations, my attention was diffused and she took advantage of it.'

'You never got to the bookshop,' said Mrs Strumbold dangerously.

'Madam,' I expostulated, 'it was quite impossible. I couldn't let her go without a word or gesture of dissent. It would have been unmanly. Besides, think of the awkwardness. It alters all our plans. Just when things were going on so nicely and a successful conclusion to our trials seemed on the point of arriving. You cannot imagine how put out I am.'

'I was looking forward to a good read,' said Mrs Strumbold. 'I'm old now. I haven't much to hope for in this world. My back's been terrible the whole day. But I thought that as it was Tuesday I should have something to cheer me up before going to bed.'

'How can I help it?' I cried in despair, gazing down into malevolent eyes. 'The shops had shut by the time I'd given up the search. I traversed many streets. I owed it to you to be thorough. She's your granddaughter.'

'Uh,' said Mrs Strumbold.

'On several occasions I thought I saw her vanishing round a corner. Her coat was blowing out behind her. But I was mistaken. Either it proved to be somebody else — in one case black, in another Arabian — or else it turned out to have been a mere trick of the imagination, caused by anxiety for your comfort and convenience, madam.'

'Well, I don't blame her for wanting a change of air,' said Mrs Strumbold. 'What's for supper? It's late.'

I went into the kitchen. It seemed the best thing to do in these miserable circumstances. With a special key I'd had made, I opened the old woman's drink cupboard as quietly as possible.

'What are you doing?' she shouted.

'Getting out the milk,' I replied instantly. 'I invented a new recipe on the way home. I'm sure you'll like it. Guaranteed to give satisfaction to all types of palate. A succulent variation on a traditional dish of the steppes. Eaten by Genghiz Khan. Relished by subsequent Asiatic potentates, including Stalin.'

'I believe you're at my whiskey,' she yelled.

'Oh, have you any?' I enquired brightly, feeling very much the better for my nip. Confidence began returning to me. I even imagined myself getting the upper hand. 'I thought the cupboard was bare. Now do be a sweet old Grandma and lend me the key for a second. A dash of whiskey in my recipe would lift it into the super luxury class. Let us pretend to be rich for this evening. Any psychologist will tell you it's the perfect treatment for persons recently stunned by bad news. Even those of low intelligence and limited imagination are dependent on things of the mind. It's what differentiates us from the brute creation.' I clattered saucepans and plates.

'Don't waste my declining years with these damned lies,'

she screamed. 'How much have you had and how did you open the cupboard? I've got the key round my neck with my money.'

'Some of my friends are crooks,' I sang, taking another pull. 'I cultivate them for professional reasons. Local colour. Inside information. One wants to be able to vary one's characters. It's dull to have them all the same class, for example. One should be able to go down the scale as well as up. But how am I to hobnob with the rich,' I cried despondingly, 'if Nancy's absence means I've got to waste my precious time earning wages? If my masterpieces and, consequently, my fame are to be postponed indefinitely by that cruel girl? She is not a Strumbold for nothing.'

'Pretty near,' said Grandma. 'Put that bottle back at once.'

I complied, in order to appease her. I wanted her in a good humour and ready to advise on the most expeditious method of getting my darling to return. The light flashed on glass necks and shoulders as I shut the door. I began pacing the kitchen, occasionally sipping from a small cup I had taken the precaution to fill and place behind the clock.

'It's not that I'm ignorant of society life,' I remarked. 'During my newspaper days, I was often assigned to hot-spots, weddings, hunt balls and the arrival of celebrities at airports. I took my work seriously, giving it my full attention and enquiring into the background, tastes, potentialities and future plans of everyone coming to my notice.'

'What about some food?' said Mrs Strumbold.

'I'm laying the table,' I replied, hastily tinkling a handful of forks. 'But what I now fear is that I've got out of date. The rich are always bustling about, trying to find new ways of wasting time and money. It's a terrible problem for them.'

'Never suffered from it myself,' said Mrs Strumbold.

'Yes,' I cried, as if addressing a news conference, 'they grapple with this conundrum day and night. It oppresses them. They get neurotic. Doctors fatten on them. New forms of night life are invented in the hope that they may enjoy themselves, temporarily at least and at the greatest possible expense. New beaches, replete with casinos, swimming-pools, polo, water ski-ing, girls of all shapes and colours, are promoted by ingenious persons on the make. Believe me, madam, millions are sunk in the enterprise of fleecing the rich.'

'You're not thinking of going into the hotel business?' Mrs Strumbold enquired. 'Now that Nancy's cleared out?'

'No, no, no,' I screeched, seizing the cup behind the clock. 'What I'm trying to say is that I must be free to conduct my researches into significant aspects of the age in my own way. I, too, am in the entertainment business. But not as an employee because it doesn't suit my temperament and it also wastes my gifts. I shall certainly make immense quantities of money in the end. Any business or professional enterprise takes time to get established. Do you believe in me or not, Mrs Strumbold?'

'I never had a better cook in the house,' said she appreciatively.

'Well then,' I cried, 'we must pull together. We must stand shoulder to shoulder. In other words, we must economize a little until we get Nancy back. It's out of the question for me to earn wages. We've agreed that would be a short-sighted policy, haven't we? Earning a few pounds a week now to the exclusion of the great riches we shall certainly enjoy hereafter.'

'Don't forget I'm over ninety,' remarked Mrs Strumbold. 'Hereafter must be pretty close for me.'

'You are indestructible, madam,' I replied warmly. 'As a

student of human nature, I can assure you of it. You are not of the species *Homo sapiens* at all, but belong to some other order of beings, as yet unclassified by science. Unknown to anyone except me.'

'I know, I know,' said the old woman, suddenly appearing at the kitchen door. She was now very tottery and hunched almost double. She wore a wig of red curls as her hair had almost gone. Her eyes were as sharp as ever under the drooping lids. 'You've said it all before,' she added, squinting up into my face as well as the rigid state of her neck allowed. 'You talk too much. I don't wonder Nancy ran for it.'

'How shall I get her back?' I demanded, overcome by grief. 'The equilibrium here was so delicately and satisfactorily poised. She is a wicked woman.'

'Nonsense,' said Mrs Strumbold. 'She hasn't the guts for that.'

I took the old creature by the shoulders and shook her briskly to emphasize my words. The sequins flashed on the low-cut evening dress she'd put on in order to enjoy fully the book I ought to have bought with her old-age pension. The shawl fell off her crooked back, but I took no notice, shouting into her best ear: 'Economy! Economy! Economy! It's the only thing left for us now. You'll have to read the old books for a bit. Why, there must be nearly a hundred, not counting what you inherited from your late lamented husband.'

'I know them off by heart,' she panted, as well as she was able. 'I'm too old to have my pleasures cut down. What sort of a world is it if you haven't the right to enjoy yourself even at ninety-one? Why, when I was your age, nobody thought of stinting his grandmother-in-law. Other members of the family took the pinch first. It was considered the right thing to do,' she gasped indignantly, struggling from my grip and leaning against the whiskey cupboard.

'You'll have to drink less, too,' I muttered, stooping over her stunted form. 'Are we to starve and freeze and sit in the dark until Nancy comes back? Because she will come back in the end. Won't she?'

'What else can she do?' said Mrs Strumbold sourly.

'Yes, yes,' I cried, taking the cup from behind the clock, drinking half a teaspoonful and handing the other half to my companion. 'She must. She will. My life depends on it. It's impossible to imagine oneself being deserted in this way. I love her so much, so deeply, so truly. Everything about her increases my passion. Her silences, for instance; her timidity; the fact that she is incapable of understanding my aspirations. Perhaps it was her longing to be free that attracted me most. Oh, I can't begin to explain. I mean, it would take too long for an impatient nature like yours.' I began breaking eggs into the fryingpan and thrusting slices of bread under the grill. I poured in old vegetables and dried up bits of ham and mixed it vigorously with a fork. Mrs Strumbold sniffed.

'I shall search until I find her,' I continued, almost at random in my distress. 'Surely she will be drawn to our favourite haunts. The places where we used to sit down free of charge and talk whenever the weather was clement. Maybe it was her virtues as a listener which bound me to her. For that was a lack I had felt rather sharply in my previous life. People have such a tendency to contradict. They think it adds to the intellectual content of a discourse. They have an idea that one ought to debate.'

'You've forgotten to put in the pepper,' said Mrs Strumbold, opening the cupboard and bringing out the last full bottle.

'Oh, madam,' I cried feverishly, 'you are much more

intuitive than a casual acquaintance might suppose. It is perfectly right to celebrate the beginning of a great quest. I shall scour even the places we only visited once or twice in an extravagant mood. Who knows, she might be more drawn to them than to the others, even though we loved them better because we felt at ease and the sun was warm. Women are not easily understood. They have their own system of logic. Not that I criticize.'

We sat opposite each other at the small table. Mrs Strumbold's meagre bosom glittered with the movements of her knife and fork and particularly as she raised her glass in salute, saying: 'Hard times are coming. Bear up. You'll be ninety-one soon enough and then you won't mind so much.'

'That is a long way off, thank God,' I replied in some horror. 'There is much to be done first. Shall we have another drink before the sober days set in?'

'Agreed,' said she, taking off the cap with alacrity.

She seemed in amazing spirits and I wondered whether she might have a store of sovereigns under the floorboards. 'Madam,' I said cautiously, 'in our present painful circumstances, we ought to be absolutely frank with each other. It is time to do our accounts, in short to declare our assets, overt and concealed.'

'Cheese,' said Mrs Strumbold.

I reached behind me and placed it in front of her, continuing, 'By working like a maniac, I can finish my new book in two months and get an advance. While resting from these severe mental labours, I could take a job in a hotel as night cook. It will be the season for dances, dinners, outings and similar jollifications.'

'I recommended the hotel business quite ten minutes ago,' remarked Mrs Strumbold, devouring hard cheese and whiskey. What a digestion!

'This new book will certainly be a success,' I cried with the utmost enthusiasm. 'I've put everything into it: rich people, perversion, sudden death, love, drama—'

'Food?' asked Mrs Strumbold contentedly.

'Rare foods, exciting drinks, drugs, lunacy, corruption. How can I fail this time? It's not artificial, either. I feel strongly on all these subjects. I admire the rich. Perversion thrills me. Why are you wearing that extraordinary red wig tonight?'

'To celebrate Nancy's departure,' she said, filling my glass.

'And that fetching gown,' I said deliriously. 'Oh, you are the most dreadful old horror it has been my fortune to meet. Do you know, as I came along in the bus, I actually wondered whether it would be worse to lose you, or my darling, my love, the only woman who has ever stirred me beyond mere curiosity. That's why we must stick together, not spending your money on spirits or dirty books until I can find Nancy again.'

'Perhaps you won't,' said Mrs Strumbold, draining her glass.

'I will, I swear I will,' I returned, as though some threat had been made to me. 'My life depends on her as well as you. She must come back. I shall search the country during my time off from cooking. I shall advertise. When the money begins to come in from my book — from films, television, serials and so on — I shall employ agents to track her down. She shan't escape for long, I promise you,' I shouted, leaning over Mrs Strumbold with a knife and fork in my hand.

'As if it mattered,' she grumbled, yawning prodigiously. 'Such a boring damnfool of a girl. Have you a pencil?'

I gave her one and she marked the whiskey and put it back in the cupboard. 'Must economize,' she grunted.

'Must keep clear in the head in order to concentrate on literature and love. The trouble is that at my age you've heard it all before.'

With that, she suddenly sank down under the table, and I had difficulty in dragging her out. Handfuls of sequins came off her dress wherever I gripped it. For a moment I wondered whether she might not be some moth-eaten old waxwork, but that was only the effect of whiskey, I believe. I was unaccustomed to more than surreptitious little nips once in a way. Of course she was alive. I got her in my arms at last. Perhaps the knife and fork, still gripped in my left fist, had impeded my movements. I threw them on to the draining-board, saying: 'Come now, madam, none of this play-acting, if you please. My nerves are sufficiently on edge without that. I have worries an amoral person like you can hardly conceive of. Open your eyes, for heaven's sake.'

She was as light and as limp as an old sack. Her bones seemed to rattle together inside her skin. The wig fell off. The gown came to pieces. Fortunately she wore very stout coarse underclothes. Her skin was ancient leather and nothing less than barbed wire would have irritated it. How I envied her. I always had to have such expensive vests and pants in order to avoid coming out in blotches. It had often been a severe drain on my purse.

She lay awkwardly in my embrace as I struggled up the stairs, which had a sudden right-hand turn four steps from the top. I determined to rub out the mark on the bottle, replacing it a couple of inches lower down. I would also collect the best-illustrated dirty books from her desk and sell them to a certain shy fellow I'd met hanging about outside a number of shops and peep shows. We could not afford to have spare capital like that lying there unconverted.

'Here we are,' I said jovially, kicking her bedroom door ajar. 'It's time to wake up now because I'm certainly not going to put you into your nightgown. It's beyond the polite duty expected of a prospective grandson-in-law. Not that I wish to stand on my dignity in any unsuitable way. Far from it. I'm all for the unconventional life, for live and let live, for non-interference and the blessings of independent thought.'

I shook her pretty sharply, in the hope of rousing consciousness. The only result was that her head twisted sideways and her mouth dropped open. 'Obstinate old fool!' I shouted, pitching her on to the bed. 'The maximum of trouble! Expense! A deliberate trial. Perhaps you think of yourself as a punishment for my sins? If so, it's grossly unfair. I'm convinced I've never done half as many wicked acts as you. Why, I'm hopelessly innocent, for one thing. Even after three years of your tuition. Who knows how many more my servitude will last?' I added in a sombre tone, high spirits ebbing all at once.

I poked her and she gave no sign of life. I bent over her, but there was such a roaring and throbbing in my head that it was impossible to hear whether she breathed. Unable to decide if she was suffering from drink, a stroke, or had actually passed on to better worlds, I sat on the bed, took her hand and addressed her thus: 'Madam! What is the nature of heaven? Is it a place of eating, drinking, dancing and love, as supposed by various pagan systems? A habitat, my dear Grandma, where you would be young enough to enjoy all these things again, yet not so young that you couldn't appreciate the very special nature of the blessings conferred? Or is it a limbo from which the pleasures of the flesh have evaporated and only those of the mind remain intact, enhanced with a vigour hardly to be imagined by mere human beings?'

I tugged her fingers and tried to open one of her eyes. 'Are you dead or not?' I whispered intently. 'Give me a sign. I insist. The question is important and must be settled one way or the other before I go to bed. It would be hard to sleep in such circumstances. So many things are contingent on whether you're alive. Would my Nancy come back sooner if she knew you'd been disposed of? She might admire me more. I believe one of the difficulties between us is that she thinks I don't consider her comfort enough—though God knows, that's absolutely false. I think of little else from day to day. Or perhaps it is rather that she finds me unmanly. I've tried to explain that's simple lack of experience on her part. She will read women's magazines and how can any real person be expected to conform to those serial dreams? She won't listen to reason, or anything else I can think of,' I remarked disconsolately, slapping my companion sharply on both cheeks.

This seemed to work better than previous treatment. I continued briskly for several minutes. She gave a gasp, and then a shudder. I could definitely see she was breathing. I put another pillow under her head and, after some thought, one to support her ankles. I covered her with a blanket right up to the chin and stuffed the wig into the cupboard.

'It was a glorious party,' I murmured, leaning on the door. 'There's much to be said for departing this life at the end of one's last bottle of whiskey. But it is evidently not your destiny. I wish I knew whether your recovery is good for my prospects with Nancy. One can never tell how it will please a woman to behave. It depends on what part of the magazine dream they're possessed by. That is to say, women like my darling.'

I stopped my monologue as if choked. Was it really true that Mrs Strumbold interested me more than you?

17

'No, that I will never believe,' wrote Joseph furiously, his pen flying along the lines at indecipherable speed. 'It's just not true that I came to value you simply for your grandma, remarkable though she was. Why, the whole history I'm writing proves the contrary. That's the reason I labour at it, day in, day out. To prove my love, my sanity, and also my genius, of course.'

He got up and saw there was such a blizzard raging that the road and everyone on it was completely invisible. The furthermost object he could discern was the shape of a laurel bush three-quarters of the way down the path to the gate, on the right. The house was full of howling and whistling which might have been the wind, though he was inclined to doubt it. There was rustling everywhere, as of papers moving, settling, sliding, shifting. Or it might be rats. Or rats masticating enormous mounds of paper which slithered as they swung their jaws and twitched their tails.

The hammering had decreased, he was glad to note. It had been a particularly disturbing manifestation, mainly because it was not regular, but started suddenly as if in his very ears, and then died away, leaving him straining for last echoes in the silence, all concentration destroyed. The rats were infinitely preferable, even though they might be eating something very important: facts, or lists of objects it was essential for him to know if his studies were to be brought to a successful conclusion, as they must be. He had resolved on that at least.

Yet, if he lived a hundred years, he could not hope to read more than a small part — say twenty-five per cent — of the mysterious literature by which he was engulfed. What a lucky man he was. So many people suffered tortures of boredom simply from not having enough to do and from that which they had being repetitive, uninteresting and altogether beneath contempt. He had been preserved from that fate.

He took up his pen with an enthusiastic gesture and began to write while the snow drifted deeper in the garden, covering the bushes and the brambles as though with sheets of paper. The flakes swirling down reminded him of torn up manuscripts descending into a basket.

But he must not allow his attention to wander, soothed by unaccustomed quiet. Everything had stopped. Now was his chance to get on, to explain. There were lacunae in his narrative which had the effect of throwing doubt on his motives and giving rise to gossip in the neighbourhood. It was necessary to repair them. Not that people would ever accept an innocent explanation of a good story. How was he to know that Mrs Strumbold was not suffering from the effects of drink, but had had a stroke? He was not sober enough, for one thing. Nor was he a medical man, accustomed to divine the proper meaning of limpness, paleness, twitchings, no matter how inebriated the patient. It was most unreasonable to suppose he could, or should.

Yet people had done so. They pointed out that Nancy had disappeared on the very day the poor old woman had sunk unconscious on to the floor, where she had been left, they said, the whole night in the hope that she would die. Many theories were propounded as to what had brought on her seizure. Of course, she was ninety-one, but hale and hearty and not showing signs of imminent collapse. Joseph had certainly caused this, perhaps through negligence, but more likely from malice and a desire to possess himself of the old woman's property. When she eventually did die, it was found that she had willed everything to him.

If more proof of funny work were needed, people said, one had only to cite Nancy's subsequent history. Joseph, however, was diabolically clever — probably these were by no means his first crimes — and nothing could be pinned on him legally. Everyone read his books with avidity, recognizing poor old Mrs Strumbold here, and poor daft Nancy there. It was possible to put two and two together to a certain extent, but never sufficiently. One could only watch and listen, hoping for supplementary clues. Orgies took place. That was indisputable. Toby the vanman had seen naked girls through the letter-box.

It was also believed that Joseph had been terribly disfigured, either by acid, fire, or the effects of general wickedness. As no one had laid eyes on him for a long time, the question remained open. Toby said he had a great scar running right across his forehead, down between the eyebrow and the hair and a good way on to the cheek. On the other hand, one had to allow for the fact that Toby was a well-known liar and exaggerator. But there might be something in what he said. At least, it could not be denied that Nancy came to grief and Mrs Strumbold had a stroke and no doctor was called until the next morning. Also, one mustn't forget the favourable will, under the terms of which Joseph inherited The Nook and everything it contained, lock, stock and barrel. The Qwikcleen salesman had been much struck by this last point and he was a man greatly experienced in the ways of the world, on account of his profession.

Joseph was aware of all these stories from the many

anonymous letters and telephone calls he had received. These had been fairly evenly divided between the drunken, abusive and falsely sympathetic, who hoped by sweetness and a pretended indignation against scandal-mongers to get at the truth. For it was generally agreed that this was far stranger and more shocking than anything related by Toby. It was stronger stuff than they had in the Sunday newspapers. The fact that Joseph was almost entirely invisible and the house exuded an air of solitude and total neglect proved it. Was it natural to live like that unless one had something to hide? Especially in the case of a man whose books were in the public library and whose voice had been heard over the wireless several times.

'I hope my darling will forgive me,' Joseph anxiously thought, 'for having caused all this absurd speculation about us. No doubt it could have been avoided if I had made a point of going round the public houses on Saturdays and joining in local theatricals. But, apart from the extreme boredom of such a programme, life is too short for irrelevancies. Why, I hardly dare to pause for food now that I've discovered what an enormous amount of research remains to be done before a proper statement can be arrived at. Every day the work increases, no matter how industrious I am.'

He bent quickly over his task, in order by concentration to obliterate the movements at the bottom of the stairs. It had grown dark and the lamp shone obliquely over his face, filling his eyes with shadows and casting his nose in relief above the twilight region where his lips lay fluttering slightly. The snow drifting on the window-sill gleamed and sparkled through the glass and frostferns grew upon the upper panes. Joseph wrote on and on. It was not possible to tell how many hours were passing: all the clocks in the house had long since stopped.

145

18

I TOOK the postcard up from the mat and read: 'Have
met an enormous Swede.'

'News! News!' I shouted, rushing up to Mrs Strumbold's bedroom. 'She's written at last to inform me of a
meeting with a Swede of large dimensions. But whether she
refers to his height, his breadth, or some other character-
istic, is not fully explained. Perhaps she means enormously
wealthy.'

'Shouldn't think so,' remarked Mrs Strumbold, perusing
the card with contempt. Though partially bed-ridden after
her stroke, she was in all other respects exactly the same
as before. I believed she could never have been different at any period. I had once tried to imagine her as a
little girl and as a shy young woman without the least
success.

'But what can be her object in writing in this cryptic
manner?' I demanded, pacing from the bed to the window
and back again. 'There are many other items concerning
her daily life which she knows would interest me extremely. Her address, for instance, and whether the Swede
plans to take her to Sweden, or to some warmer part of the
world, such as Spain.'

'Postmark's London,' yawned Mrs Strumbold.

'I noted that while climbing the stairs,' I returned. 'I
shall, of course, go to London later in the morning. At
what part of the metropolis do you suggest I could most

profitably begin my search? I don't want to waste more time than I can help for reasons of economy and also from principle. As you know, I've already scoured every likely place.'

'Try Scandinavian haunts,' said Mrs Strumbold. 'She especially says an enormous Swede. You might invite him to accompany her home.'

'That was not part of my plan,' I replied, taking the card from her and holding it up to the light, as though in the hope of detecting invisible messages. 'My intention is to save Nancy from the consequences of her own folly. Surely you will admit that it is most unwise for a young woman to take up with a foreigner of unusual measurements. It's my duty to do something about it,' I cried with enthusiasm, 'and I shall. Not a single Scandinavian haunt will remain uninvestigated. And I think it's a good idea to bring him back here. We want to enquire into his origins and background and find out whether he has seduced Nancy with a lot of lies; or whether it was other qualities, besides a ready tongue, that made him so captivating. I'm determined to get to the bottom of it. I don't know if it has ever struck you, madam, but Nancy remains a mysterious character, even after an extensive acquaintance. She has depths and silences of which the meaning is difficult to divine. I shall therefore enlist the help of this Swede, who may be more experienced than we think. I mean, one doesn't associate Sweden with great subtlety — those huge blond boys — but that is probably only an insular prejudice.'

'Huge blond boys, I should think so,' interpolated Mrs Strumbold, waking from a sudden doze. 'Why all this talk?'

I handed her a tin of biscuits and continued: 'Because it's essential to make up one's mind what to do before doing it. A short essay by any writer on any general would

147

demonstrate the truth of what I say. Amply. It's no good bringing this Swede here unless we have prepared a suitable questionnaire and tests of different sorts to measure his abilities, both physical and mental, with some degree of accuracy. We live in a scientific age which has provided us with tools and procedures for assessing a man's fascinations, be he blond or dark.'

'Humm-mumm,' munched Mrs Strumbold as crumbs cascaded down her chin, bounced on her bosom and settled in a fold of sheet. It was as if she devoured handfuls of live insects, ten per cent of which escaped her jaws through superior activity and general know-how.

'My proposals are entirely in the interests of literary research,' I murmured, resting against the wardrobe. 'I'm very glad to think that my sweetheart is enjoying herself in new ways she will impart to me on her return, whenever that occurs. I don't wish to cut her short, only to have more certain news. I could have a Swede as hero of my next book. It might sell better. Though the last was an improvement on the one before, so I needn't despair of my inventive powers. That fellow is not going to be given more than his fair share of credit, be his measurements what they may.'

'Hehohehoheh!' laughed Mrs Strumbold, crumbs shooting in all directions.

'You find it amusing, madam,' I shouted in a thin voice, 'but I'm deadly serious. I put on light airs simply in order not to appear conceited. But the sole reason I haven't yet set off in pursuit is that I'm not sure whether I ought to knife my successor before congratulaing my darling on her enterprise. I long to give her the greatest possible happiness.' I struck the wardrobe with my fist and the door flew open, revealing many brown paper parcels piled on top of each other.

'Oh, stab him, then,' said Mrs Strumbold, bored, 'I dare say she'd like that as well as anything. Who ate all the ones with sugar on them?'

'Who do you think?' I asked bitterly. 'When did I last have a biscuit with sugar, or butter, on it I should like to know? Who drank the end of the whiskey? I'm abstemious by nature, but you go too far. Nobody likes to be imposed on. It sets up frustrations of a disagreeable and even dangerous nature. What do all these parcels contain, for instance? I never saw them before.'

'Jewellery,' said Mrs Strumbold with a fantastic grin. 'Bank notes. Indecent memoirs. Gold.'

'How can that be true?' I urged, seizing the nearest one and grappling with the many knots by which it was secured. 'Do you claim to be concealing treasure while we pinch and save to make ends meet? While we put on overcoats and snow boots in order not to light the fire? Oh God! You must be mad.' I tore the paper off and, as I had suspected, every hope was dashed. There was nothing but rubbish inside that parcel: moth-eaten vests, tinsel shoes and celluloid pearl necklaces.

'Me mad!' cried Mrs Strumbold in a paroxysm. 'That's rich!'

Without waiting for more, I dashed down the stairs, leaving her covered with crumbs and bits of brown paper. I ran along the road in a state of confusion. The bare branches of the ornamental trees and shrubs in people's gardens were waving in an icy wind, though I didn't feel cold. Cigarette ends and the remains of cardboard boxes skidded past my feet. I had not even a penknife on me. Yet, a handkerchief was really just as good if you came up unexpectedly behind a man and twisted it round his neck. It could be done in a second. I had read accounts of thuggee in India with particular attention, though it hadn't seemed, at that time, that the information could ever be of practical use.

'But it just shows,' I muttered breathlessly, 'one should never let slip an opportunity of improving one's mind. I believe this handkerchief would be long enough, provided he isn't too fat in the neck. Is it possible that a person as fond of birds as you are, darling, could be overwhelmed by a neck padded with rolls of superfluous flesh?' I refused point blank to entertain the idea.

I got on to the bus, taking a seat over the back wheels. No other was vacant. The road was rough and I bounced like a ball in the steamy atmosphere. All the windows were misted over and one could tell where one was only by instinct and smart calculations. It might be better, I thought, to make myself known at once, assuming an air of bonhomie. Not so false as to put the Swede on his guard. I would have to be careful there because I didn't know how intelligent he was. He might be a man who could put two and two together, though the postcard gave no hint of intellectual powers.

He might, on the contrary, be a mere hulk and especially selected by my darling for that very quality. I had sometimes suspected that she lacked mental stamina. Otherwise she would surely have learnt more from our association, considering the many informative talks we had enjoyed. I myself had benefited much, both in the understanding of the feminine nature and in the clarification of subsidiary ideas on which I happened to be working. Not that I wished to criticize my darling in any way at all. Far from it. Everything she did or said enchanted me beyond measure. I was merely stating the facts as I swayed in the bus, because it was essential to have an adequate plan of campaign.

I would begin by informing the Swede of my prior claim

on Nancy, pointing out the length of our friendship and my superior qualifications: my last book had plainly indicated that I was really beginning to go ahead. The dazzling future I had always promised my sweetheart was at last about to dawn. The Swede should be left in no doubt of that. I would ask him what he had to offer. I would address him in difficult words, since it was probable that he didn't know English very well. I would have him stuttering and contradicting himself in no time.

I got off the bus and began hastening through the streets. A biting wind full of dust caught me at right-hand corners. Rows of tightly shut windows hung above my head. The lights were on behind some, I noted, although it was broad day. What a symbol of riches. I stood stock still amongst old leaves and bits of paper, lost in a sudden vision of a large interior lined with precious books: first editions, limited editions, illuminated books and sets of rare engravings. To one side was a fine antique desk with my manuscript and correspondence on it. There were easy chairs, bottles of whiskey and a Renoir over the fireplace. The whole was brilliantly lit by electric candelabra, the latest sort of desk lamp, a spotlight for the Renoir and other subsidiary lights so that there was not a dark corner anywhere. And you were lolling, fast asleep, in one of the comfortable chairs.

Oh, darling, how I ran as if there were not a moment to be lost! As if I must find you immediately in order to make this dream come true. For I knew now that the Swede was of no importance. 'Keep the fellow,' I murmured under my breath. 'I don't mind. Why should I? What has Sweden, or any place you like to mention in the Arctic Circle, to do with us? Amuse yourself as you please, my dearest. One of your problems is a tendency to low spirits. How I understand. I've struggled with it myself, often alone and in dingy circumstances. We must each find the solution that suits us best. In your case, it's this Swede. Bring him to The Nook, darling. It's much the most sensible course. Grandma is in need of new distractions. Poor health bores her because it makes her feel her age. Sometimes I can hardly cheer her, no matter how I try. It's a terrible fate to be ninety-one and right in the head.'

I passed restaurants full of people eating tasty foods, while underground, or in a cupboard somewhere out of sight, were slaves in dirty overalls washing up and washing up in the hope of paying the bills; of buying things to keep ferocious grandmothers quiet; waiting for better times to come with all the patience it was possible to summon to their help in tides of grease and open buckets overflowing with the scraping of a hundred plates.

'This is where the Swede would come in useful,' I muttered to my own reflection in a glass advertisement for tea. 'He can do the café jobs when our finances fail. I guarantee to support him during the good times. It'll work out a pretty equal *quid pro quo*. He will be the greatest asset in The Nook. I understand at last. My one regret is that you should have found this temporary absence necessary. But terminate it now, my darling, or I won't answer for the consequences.'

I was tearing through a park at a most tremendous speed. There was a lake containing fancy ducks and on the banks a number of people stood with paper bags in their hands. I would have liked to pause and meditate on the reasons by which such persons persuaded themselves that it was meritorious to transport large supplies of bread, biscuits, cake and throw them down before insatiable and undeserving birds. I would have enjoyed a leisurely examination of the psychological aspects, both avian and

152

human. Very likely, a brilliant couple of paragraphs could have been composed in other circumstances.

I hadn't a moment to spare. I was approaching the postal district stamped on your card, which I held in front of me, as though with the intention of reading it again; of tracing the convolutions of your pen across this unique space. I gripped it like a talisman, for besides the letter-box into whose mouth you had actually put your bony fingers with their bitten nails, this postal district also contained a seedy art club called Swedo-Zero. Where should I find you, if not there?

I began rehearsing my opening speech. 'Let's have a drink,' I'd say. 'Bring your friend. He looks interesting. Beer? A sandwich? Scandinavian titbit? I'll pay. Are you hungry, sir? Introduce me, darling, to our distinguished guest. We live so quietly that it's not often we have the fortune to meet men like him. Sir, you must come and visit us at The Nook. It's a comfortable and interesting address and we have a sort of spare room. Not large, you know, but adequate, convenient, private. You wouldn't be disturbed. I take it you are engaged on important work of some kind? Research? Sagas? Comparative archaeology? Forgive my curiosity. I don't mean to pry. It's just that Nancy's friends are my friends, naturally. I can't help feeling drawn to you, sir, in a strange, compelling way. May I shake your hand?'

As I neared the end of the park and prepared to enter the narrow streets by which it was surrounded, I wondered whether this was not too humble an approach. It might be better to say: 'Ah, Nancy, there you are at last. I got your card and came as quickly as I could, considering that you neglected to give me the precise address. No matter. Is this the fellow you mentioned? Explain yourself my good man, if you please. My fiancée is a nervous woman, easily imposed on. Also, she says things she doesn't mean, when driven into a corner. The feminine nature is like that. It's no use blaming her. One has to learn to accept disappointment in this life, I assure you. I speak as a man of the world. Is there anything you wish to say to him, darling, before we leave? Heavens above, what a noise there is and so much dirt on the tables and chairs. Don't think I should object to his visiting us at The Nook occasionally. You know I'm as hospitable as our means permit. But remember that you're under no obligation to be polite to him. His behaviour and general attitude forbid it.'

I hurried faster and faster, trying to decide which of these two excellent speeches to make. There was so much to recommend both. I did not, of course, want to upset my darling, only to get her back, to take her home immediately, to establish her in the proper surroundings. She had nothing Scandinavian about her. This whole adventure was a mistake. It was my duty to rescue her.

'Dearest,' it suddenly struck me that I might begin, 'I've come to save you, save you, save you. From the consequences of your own folly. From the results of misunderstanding and lack of mental grip. Oh, how much anxious thought is necessary in this life with all its unexpected ups and downs and the hordes of foreigners invading our shores under a pretence of friendship and an interest in English customs. Why should our habits be scrutinized by Swedes in particular? I believe you will regret having encouraged him. But bring him to The Nook, if you insist. At least we shall be able to keep an eye on him and prevent his worst impertinences. Because, as you must have realized long ago, sweetest, foreigners have no idea how to behave. They have no sense of values. It's quite likely he thinks of you simply as an amenable girl with whom he can pass a little time before seriously starting his career. He can't possibly have grasped the intricacies of your nature, your unique gifts, veiled as they are in almost perpetual silence. Nancy, my queen, my goddess, my muse, don't throw yourself away on a Swede.'

I was now standing on the top of the stairs leading down to Swedo-Zero. I descended. A confused noise of voices and a smell of beer and sausage rushed up from below on a strong draught. I could not distinguish my darling's nasal tones. She had never been keen on any kind of sausages except beef chipolatas. The ones here were full of onions, cloves, garlic and adulterated matter. Perhaps I would not have to face the Swede after all.

I continued downwards in a dream. These rooms had once been coal cellars and there was still a suggestion of soot in them. Very powerful lights had been fitted everywhere. Coils of cigarette smoke floated under the bulbs. Swedes, Danes, Norwegians, Negroes, Chinese, Filipinos, Americans, Germans and Britishers were sitting on the floors declaiming. I could not catch their drift. But one thing seemed certain: it was not the sort of atmosphere where my darling flourished. She was anti-intellectual to the core. That was one of my most important discoveries about her. It had not been easy to come to this conclusion on account, as I say, of the silence that buried her motives in obscurity. Buried her personality. Buried her. Buried.

I passed into a second room, less crowded since there were no refreshments to be had. Pictures and sculptures were displayed. I examined them intently. If there was anything specifically Swedish, I would make enquiries at the bar, or else from a recumbent couple who occupied the middle of the floor.

I paused in front of a sculpture consisting of a handful of nails which moved slowly in different directions, similar to the evolutions of a bunch of seaweed underwater. Every so often, they emitted a short, dry screech. I was almost over-come by a temptation to put my finger in among them.

'When one contemplates the tenderness of those lateral movements,' cried the young man at my feet in a voice of active dislike, 'the sensuality with which the nailheads coalesce and separate, one is forcibly reminded of the ele-mental dance of the atoms.'

'Bravo,' said the girl, 'Schlipperhotstein couldn't do better.'

'Shut up,' said the boy. 'God, why am I in love with an ignorant lump like you?'

'Ask Schlipperhotstein,' said the girl with a huge yawn. They kissed and settled more closely into each other's arms. A strong smell of onions rose up from them.

Ah, my darling, I mused nostalgically, why are we not like this ourselves? Even the great Schlipperhotstein, who-ever he may be, heartily recommends it. Consider the many times we have whispered together on the floor, though we never smelt of anything worse than that ex-tremely sickly soap you fancied at one period. The ad-vertisements said it gave an extra personal freshness and you believed them. We endured half a dozen tablets before Mrs Strumbold revolted.

'I'm looking for a Miss Strumbold,' I said politely to my new acquaintances. 'I have reason to believe she may be a member of this outfit on account of a certain large boy-friend by whom she has been temporarily captivated.'

'Never heard of her,' mumbled the girl.

'Does she paint, or what?' the boy demanded.

'She is not in the least artistic,' I said warmly. 'Her in-terests are domestic and personal, so far as she can be said to have any. But that's not the point. She has mysterious qualities, difficult to define at short notice. Is Schlipper-hotstein, by chance, a Swede?'

'He's too dark for a Swede,' said the girl sleepily.

'There are dark Swedes,' said the boy.

'Don't believe it,' said the girl.

'I suggest you ask the secretary,' said the boy to me. 'You'll find him behind the bar. He has a list of members. If Miss Rumbold has given her correct name, she will be on it.'

'Strumbold,' I said faintly, appalled by this new complication. If my darling was going about under false names, how could I hope to track her down, even by the exercise of superhuman assiduity? The sculpture gave a sad shriek and the fetid air enveloped me warmly, damply, like a horrible old blanket saved from a rubbish heap. 'That was her name when I knew her, at least. Could you not be slightly more helpful, my young friends? I'm no prude. You can trust me. I am in favour of enjoyment and damn the consequences. I shall not reproach her. But I must get her back — that is to say, I must make every effort to get her back. Much depends on the result of my labours. I'm at a cross-roads in my life. Left or right?' I cried hysterically. 'That is the question.'

They were now both looking at me very suspiciously, resting on their elbows and clasping each other. I was an alien here, too, that was the truth of the matter. Only with my darling and her grandma did I feel at home. So instead of telling them that my last book had been quite successful and could be said to mark the beginning of my real career, I stared down on them morosely where they lay like guardian spirits before the shrine of Schlipperhotstein. The lights threw great shadows over their cheeks.

I became aware of a feeling of intensity pulsing through these unattractive premises. It was like the hush before some great event, such as the arrival of royalty, or a typhoon. There was a dry rustling like a snake in leaves:

Sschlip-lipper-hotstein-stein-ein. How it whispered back and forth, sliding over walls and floors, lapping at the stairs where I saw a darkness, as though someone were standing round the corner, at the top. I turned to my companions, but they regarded me so severely that I refrained from opening my mouth.

I leaned vaguely in the doorway, pale thoughts of my darling revolving in my head. It seemed certain that I could not find her here, even if provided with a complete list of her assumed names. Every other possible place had been watched, searched, revisited at different seasons, hours, days of the week. Swedo-Zero represented a last wild hope, now dashed, now finished, receding into memory fast. What a relief. I swayed on my feet. I could enjoy my sweetheart in remembrance, for ever at her best. For, in the flesh, she had some very trying characteristics. All those bad periods, those irritations and interruptions were blotted out by absence.

Quite intoxicated by this sudden vision of the perfect life, I continued to gaze vacantly at the staircase. The shadow on it had darkened, as though the person above had decided to come down, had advanced to the top step and put his hand on the banisters. Rat-tat-tat. A set of quick light feet were on the boards. Round the corner came a frail elderly man with much white hair, topped by a small tweed hat, of the kind sold in expensive shops for week-ends in the country.

Two young men accompanied him and to them he said, over his shoulder: 'My dear Tom, you should go to Brasilia. Heavens, what grandeur of the human spirit. What daring. What a marriage of architecture and environment, of light and texture, mass and counter-mass. It's a superb statement from whatever angle you view it, whether lying on the ground, or standing on a roof.

Humanity is dwarfed and magnified simultaneously: it is a stupendous example of imagination made actual, tangible; of a dream captured in stone, brick, concrete, steel, wood, glass and all other materials, used to give variety of surface and emotion. Are you listening, Tom?'

'Yes, sir. I've applied for one of those travelling scholarships given by the Gustenfinger Foundation, with the intention of making Brasilia the subject of my thesis.'

'Well done,' said the master distantly. 'What have we here? Why did I come, Jack? My memory's getting worse and worse. Age creeps up on the best of us, I'm afraid.'

'You have promised to address them, sir. They have left you to choose the subject.'

'Oh, really? Well, as I've got started on Brasilia, I'd better continue. What more can they want?' He sniffed distastefully, standing on the bottom step. 'Are you the president of this organization?'

'No, sir,' I replied without a moment's hesitation. 'My business is quite different from that which you suppose. I am engaged on a hopeless quest for a lady who has changed her name — many times for all I know. I've had news that she's been enchanted by a Swede. But how can I tell whether it's true information or propaganda put out to deflect me from an apprehension of the facts? Anything's possible, once one enters the world of dreams, as you have remarked yourself in relation to the city of Brasilia. Perhaps the Swede has taken her there on a travelling scholarship and walks with her, arm in arm, between the towering perspectives, the mad confrontations and echoing views of a vision in the wilderness.'

By this speech, I cleared him off those stairs. It was not his habit to hang about while people chattered. He passed away towards the refreshment room and I rushed up into the air of everyday, making for The Nook.

19

'Mrs Strumbold! Madam!' I shouted, the door key in my hand. 'I've searched everywhere and she's not to be found. I don't think there's anything else I can do until we have more certain news. We must wait for her to communicate with us again. The clues are too slender. I believe there are hundreds of Swedes in this country, not to speak of other Scandinavians whose appearance and habits are deceptively similar to our eyes.'

'You've been long enough coming to that conclusion,' grumbled the old woman.

'Don't worry,' I said absently. I had opened a letter from my publisher which said that sales had been unexpectedly good. He enquired cordially after my new book. This confirmed my belief that I was acting in the most sensible way. Good news is the reward of right conduct.

'Is it fish?' asked Mrs Strumbold, slithering down the stairs. Her legs were slightly paralysed.

'Yes!' I cried exuberantly. 'Come into the kitchen while I tell you the day's adventures.' I dragged her after me at a good pace. My excitement was great. The publisher's letter uplifted me. I felt sure of myself and my future. 'My books are better since she went,' I exclaimed. 'They've more tension and a nervous frenzy in them that communicates itself to the reader.'

'Maybe there's something in that,' said Mrs Strumbold consideringly as I wedged her against the table to prevent her slipping sideways off the chair. 'You're definitely madder.'

'I see my way clear,' I cried. 'I see money. I brought you a bottle of whiskey as a present. I got it on tick.'

'Smart work,' said Mrs Strumbold admiringly.

'I talked it out of the grocer,' I said. 'I was in that sort of mood, having settled the Nancy question. I went to a place called Swedo-Zero and consulted Schlipperhotstein, a man expert in many directions, according to my information. He advised me that she had most probably been taken to the fabled city of Brasilia, by means of a Gustenfinger scholarship.'

'Is he a fortune teller?' Mrs Strumbold enquired, passing her tongue round her lips. 'The fish has oozed over the bottle.'

'More or less,' I said. 'But a superior one, versed in dreams and portents of all sorts. The city of Brasilia is a vision in the jungles of the new world. Everyone artistic believes in it. Millions have been spent on enormous vistas crowned by banqueting halls, concert halls, and halls for exhibitions of significance. Not only that, but there are immense apartments for rich pots and for government activities. Every kind of business is carried on with the greatest avidity and miles of corridors with offices attached have been provided. Would you credit it, Mrs Strumbold, not a stick, not a stone, not a chair, tap, coathanger, saucepan is of conventional design?'

'Huh,' said Mrs Strumbold. 'What a paradise.' She had got hold of the bottle, which I thought I had placed out of her reach at the other end of the table. 'Need more medicine,' she muttered slyly. 'Feel bad today. In the legs. In the back. Across the bosom.'

'Really, madam,' I expostulated, 'if you take such large doses as that it won't last long. I can't guarantee to replace it immediately.'

'Thought you said better days had come,' she remarked contentedly. 'Tell me more about this heaven Nancy's gone to. I suppose the books are highly inspired?'

'That is so,' I agreed. 'Illustrated by the best artists, text by the most skilful writers, printing, paper and presentation a miracle of expense.'

'But as it's paradise, everyone is very rich, no doubt. what sort of postcard do you think Nancy will send us next?'

'Next postcard?' I repeated in a sudden gloom. I had been quite carried away by a delightful sense of freedom from worry and responsibility. My darling's prolonged absence had made our relationship ethereal, reminiscent.

'Postcard from heaven,' mumbled the old woman. 'But she's too straitlaced to appreciate her luck.'

I put plates on the table and they rattled a bit because my hands were trembling.

'Oh, if I had her opportunities,' sighed Mrs Strumbold, 'old age wouldn't be such a boring business. If I had a visit to paradise with a large Swede to brood on. The trouble is, one lives too long. Everyone ought to make a point of dying before becoming a nuisance.'

I gave her a large helping and sat down, filled with the voluptuous thought that my darling might be dead. Not that I wished her any ill. I slashed a corner off the butter and smoothed it tenderly over my fish lying on the plate, waiting to be devoured. I remembered my desire to swallow my love whole the first time I met her. Because, sweetheart, I ruminated, I want you to be mine, mine, mine. Wholly and entirely mine, so that you couldn't think the shortest thought without my knowing of it. You always had many reservations and I never knew what they were. But as a memory, darling, as my own personal ghost, we could start a new life together.

'Of course, I've had adventures,' Mrs Strumbold remarked, her knife and fork in either fist pointing at the ceiling. 'I don't want you to imagine I've been timid, or prudish. But actual paradise, no, it just didn't come my way.'

I emptied the saucepan over her plate. I could populate an indefinite number of books with my darling as a ghost. I felt sure of it. The publisher's letter crackled in my pocket. I would have liked to take it out again and re-read it, several times, but was afraid of what Mrs Strumbold would say. Many ideas occurred to me even now, as I sat, hastily pouring myself a drink before the bottle was too far gone and we were obliged, for reasons of economy, to put it into the cupboard. I would depict our relationship as it was, had been, could be, might have been, in the utmost detail; with a transforming fancy. It would be tremendously profitable. I should see to that.

'Once one begins to make money,' I informed Mrs Strumbold in a pious tone, 'the rest's easy. The thing snowballs. Hey presto! Rich. Famous. Dreams come true.'

'I shan't see much of it,' Mrs Strumbold retorted. 'Dreams! What next? Let's go out somewhere. I've been stuck here all day while you've been hobnobbing with that foreigner you mentioned.'

'Schlipperhotstein? Oh, he wasn't foreign. Only his name. Perhaps he's really called Williams and took the other for business reasons. I can't understand why my darling was deceived by such a fraud. After all the opportunities she's had of improving her mind. For I think I can claim without conceit to be better educated than she is. Or has been,' I murmured softly. 'How do I know whether the fabled city to which she had removed is actually situated on this earth? I had a feeling in that basement among those onions that an important message was being delivered. I spoke to Schlipperhotstein as an equal, too. He seemed to expect it. He made way for me to go up the stairs.'

Mrs Strumbold did not listen to my harangue, although she might well have profited by it. She had struggled into a fur coat, made from the backs of inexpensive animals, such as rabbits or cats. It was moth-eaten, especially round the neck. But she had fastened it tightly to keep out the draughts and pulled a crochet bonnet over her head. It had daisies embroidered in red wool on the crown. She was now struggling to get her feet into an ancient pair of snow boots. Her legs would not obey her wishes and slid backwards and forwards over the floor.

I knelt and seized her calves, saying: 'What do you want to go out for? It's much too late and much too cold. You'll catch your death.' I zipped up the boots.

'It's only half-past nine,' she said, 'and a lovely moon. Besides, would either of us care if I caught my death?'

'I shall miss you greatly, madam, when the sad day comes,' I replied following her as she hobbled with amazing speed towards the shed where her wheelchair was kept. She was wonderful over short distances. We traversed the garden in single file. Some of the brambles with which it was overgrown stuck in her cat's fur. With a courteous gesture, I disentangled her, saying: 'Allow me, please.'

She sat down in the chair and I wrapped her in a rug I had in my hand. 'The air is keen,' I remarked. 'We oughtn't to stay out long.'

'At ninety-one you can do what you like,' she replied. 'Push.'

I grasped the handle behind the crochet bonnet and we started along the footpath leading past our back gate, through the churchyard to the river. The moon was almost bright enough to read by. The ground was roughish and as she was being thrown about in the chair, I took an old clothes line from my pocket and secured her firmly.

We continued through the dreamy light for a few yards without speaking. From here one could see the upper decks of buses gliding along as if swimming on the tops of the hedges. The people inside were clearly visible, staring in front of them like waxworks. All the roofs shone blue as glass. One had a sensation of being under water.

'I understand,' I remarked, 'that there are many strange creatures, as yet unclassified by science, living on the ocean bed. The inhabitants of bathyscaphes, looking out of the windows at enormous depths, have found themselves being stared at by huge phosphorescent eyes. They have seen vast black figures of no particular shape, comfortably settled in the darkness and silence of those countries. The pressure is tremendous in such deeps. I forget the exact equation. It is much greater than that supported by a tomb.'

I opened the churchyard gate and wheeled her in. Under this light the tower looked immemorial and full of ghosts. One could see the clock plainly. It was five to ten. The gravestones stood on either side of us. Some were eighteenth-century, decorated with a cherub's head framed in wings above an elegant inscription. Some had rusty iron railings, related to old-fashioned bedsteads with brass knobs. Some were embellished with glass domes containing wax flowers that glimmered faintly like fretwork bones. There was one stone angel and a number of white marble crosses.

I felt exhilarated. 'I shall die rich and without heirs,' I cried. 'I shall leave directions for an immense memorial with angels, crosses, domes, railings and an inscription from one of the Roman satirists. I shall live in it as a ghost with my darling in perpetual bliss.'

'I shall be cremated,' said Mrs Strumbold, the words

muffled in fur. Her chin had sunk down inside her collar.

A very long, thin, combined shadow stretched before us as we passed the side of the church where a quantity of coke was stacked. It had an acrid smell, which hung in the night's still beauty.

'I remember the moonlight in the tropics,' said Mrs Strumbold to my surprise. 'I remember the enormous stars above the trees when we anchored in the river mouths at dark.'

'Perhaps I shall go east one day,' I murmured, 'though I doubt it, somehow. The new romanticism is fixed in towns and suburbs.'

'That's only your ignorance,' said Mrs Strumbold. 'I remember the phosphorescent sea. I woke up one night and looked over the side and there I saw a shoal of fish swimming round the anchor chain, all the colour of moon-light.'

'Conrad could do it,' I complained. 'But it's out of the question now.'

I was filled with astonishment at Mrs Strumbold's mood. It was as if the mound of coke had been inspired to take a scent of roses, lilies-of-the-valley, violets. Her face was in deep shadow. I could not discern more than the outline of her nose above the fur. She resembled an animal as yet unknown to science, of uncertain shape and character.

When we came to the river bank, I stopped and leaned idly on the handle at the back of the chair. One or two wisps from her blue wig had escaped from under the bonnet. I could feel them against my fingers. They were scratchy and wiry and I wondered what they were made of. Dyed horsehair? Sacking? Fine straw? Coconut fibre?

A mist was rising on the water in layers and patches, floating above the current, which ran black and fast against the bridge. One could hear it gurgling on the piles and past the bows of several boats moored opposite to where we were.

'Once I saw a shark,' growled Mrs Strumbold. 'Once I saw a shooting star. But that sort of thing is so banal. Nancyish. I hear pagoda bells. Heh-heh-huglog.' She choked.

I took her by the collar and shook her gently, but firmly, in order to dislodge the obstruction, thinking, as I worked, that there *was* something banal about my darling. I had often felt it, dismissing the idea at once as unworthy of the great love she inspired in me. For that passion was not dying down, or shrinking from absence, neglect and pre-occupation with literary matters. On the contrary, it had grown so large and powerful as to engulf me entirely. Everything she did had always fascinated me.

'Yes, yes,' I cried, rattling Mrs Strumbold in a frenzy. 'I've been possessed by her. Now that she's dead or gone for ever — it's much the same from my point of view — I'm a different person, a new man. It's most likely that she's dead, isn't it? I'd have found her in one of our haunts if it were not so. I'd have met with news, or clues, or intimations of a significant kind during my search. Because I kept it up a long time in order to be quite sure of my conclusions. Many people have been badly tripped up by careless research. As for the postcard and the Swede, I don't think we should attach too much importance to them. It's never possible to explain every item in a mystery. One can only hope to make sense of a story in a general way. Madam, madam,' I stammered, embracing her strongly while a burning sensation spread through my body. 'Was there ever any Nancy? Was she a dream? Has it always only been just us two? Together in The Nook, filling all the rooms like smoke?'

The mist had spread over the whole river from bank to

bank, and was beginning to curl up from the grass round the wheels of Mrs Strumbold's chair. I let go of her and she lay still as a heap of old clothes. The coat had risen to her ears and buried her face as far as the eye sockets.

'Why should Schlipperhotstein give himself such airs?' I demanded, struggling to direct a cooling stream of intellectual thought upon the heat of my emotions. 'Of what importance is it if one arrives underground, at Swedo-Zero for instance, dressed in a small tweed hat, accompanied by acolytes and bursting with presumption? I ask simply because it seems to have a bearing on my own predicament. Am I a fraud, or is he? Not me, not me,' I sang with the utmost conviction. 'I've reached a new beginning. Are you listening?'

I bent down and tried to look into her face, but could see nothing, though the moon was as bright as ever. It struck me, for some reason, that I ought not to have brought the old woman out on such a cold damp night. Yet it was not my fault. She had insisted and would have made an abominable row if I had attempted to argue. Unfortunately, I had no witnesses on my side. Would people believe that I had been her slave right up to the last moment? I wanted to put my hand under her chin and tip her head back and find out whether her eyes were open. If they were shut, was she asleep?

I would have liked a second opinion here; someone to take a statement on the spot so that the truth of these happenings could be preserved, no matter what was said afterwards. For I knew that The Nook was surrounded by enemies. I had seen them standing at the gate, half behind the hedge, staring and staring at the windows. All these people were against me. I recognized it clearly and, indeed, had refrained from speaking to any of them simply on that account. I didn't wish to commit myself on the smallest point. Nevertheless, I now desired a friendly witness to smooth my passage into the new life which was waiting for me at The Nook.

I seized the handle of Mrs Strumbold's chair and swung it round. The mist had suddenly increased and now carpeted the valley to a depth of approximately four feet. I could not see the ground and only Mrs Strumbold's bonnet was caught by the steely moon. It was even possible to distinguish the daisies embroidered on the crown.

The tops of the gate posts leading into the churchyard were still visible. I steered towards them carefully, saying: 'My dear madam, you are utterly indestructible. I have had many proofs of it. Look at the way you recovered from your stroke, for instance, with the minimum of doctoring. Consider your digestion, your appetite. They are those of a woman of forty — no I mean twenty. Then there is the enormous energy required to sustain your ferocious disposition. Ninety-one is a great age, it's true, but many have passed beyond it safely. What could be more natural than your dropping off to sleep on such a calm and lovely night? Why, I feel quite somnolent myself. Ha!'

We had run off the path into a low bush. The wheels of the chair seemed to be entangled in branches. The impact shook Mrs Strumbold lower into her coat, as though she were a worn-out bolster being settled into a case. Her bonnet, no longer catching the light, became a blurred shape, a sponge or similar object glimpsed beneath the ripples of a quiet sea. I dragged the chair sharply backwards and forwards, for I had a great disinclination to submerge myself alongside Mrs Strumbold and disentangle the wheels by hand. It was probably a hawthorn or a bramble bush in any case. I would get covered with blood. At last, I freed it. I could just see the old woman like a heap of seaweed below me.

169

'Madam,' I said in a reasonable voice as we proceeded, 'rouse yourself, do, from these delightful slumbers. It is a pity to miss the extraordinary effect of the mist lapping round the church like a flood. It's quite theatrical. The tops of the tombstones resemble people swimming in rows. I never saw such a thing in my life before.'

I would have enlarged on this aspect, with suitable allusions and references, had the chair not violently struck an obstacle of some sort. By a supreme effort, I managed to prevent Mrs Strumbold being tipped on to the ground. The idea of having to grope for her and stuff her back into the seat horrified me.

'We'll soon be back now,' I continued in a trembling voice. 'A little nightcap would do us good. We'll turn on the fire and have it together. Oh, what an amazing day this has been. It has inspired me. I believe I could write a whole series of books describing recent events from different points of view. I should like to outline the plots. You are such a good critic. So trenchant. So down to earth. If only Nancy had had your head. Not that I could have loved her more than I did. Please believe me, Mrs Strumbold, she was the passion of my life. I shall never experience anything like it again. I know I shan't. She seemed to create something in me which I wouldn't otherwise have possessed. How badly I express myself. Words adulterate meaning.'

My cheeks were lined with tears as I pushed steadily along the white avenue between the tombstones, the tops of which were now barely perceptible, as though the rows of swimmers had sunk beneath the surface exhausted by their efforts to keep alive. The lights of cars on the road beyond seemed to be a shoal of fishes' eyes, darting after invisible prey. Only the passengers on the top decks of the buses remained plain and sharp-cut to my anguished view.

I examined them minutely. Suppose my darling were travelling to the stop round the corner at this instant? Even if she had started from Swedo-Zero, the fare was only six and six. As the people were sitting in fours, one beside the other, it was impossible to make out the more distant faces clearly. One could only say that they all seemed as silent and motionless as corpses.

'Madam!' I cried in a high tone, 'there are moments when I suffer abominably from nerves. It's the artistic temperament. For God's sake give me a sign. Raise your hand. Move your foot — no, that's no good, the mist's too thick. But you could kick the chair; I'd feel the vibration through the handle. I don't guarantee to hear anything because there's a strange roaring in my ears. I don't know how it can have happened on a night of such still and perfect beauty as we now enjoy together. Yet, so it is. Like a great swell breaking on a beach. I should be obliged if you would explain to me why the near prospect of a life without obligations, with sufficient money and unending leisure to devote to the promotion of my own happiness should cause me so much grief. Speak to me, Mrs Strumbold, I insist.' But she would not open her lips nor move a finger to alleviate my distress.

'Come now,' I said, trying to smother my feelings with a steady voice, 'don't tease me any more. I know it amuses you to be unkind. We all have our less agreeable side. I'm not complaining. On the contrary, I suggest we celebrate Nancy's good fortune in acquiring a satisfactory lover. Who wants to be put down as a prude or killjoy? Not you, I'm perfectly certain. Well then, let's get out the whiskey as soon as we can. I'll sing you a few of those old ballads you're so fond of. The ones with unusual choruses. No one will overhear if we're careful to shut the windows and draw the curtains.'

I began to hum one of these special songs under my breath in the hope of rousing her to make a definite sign. How I longed for some acerbity to bubble through the mist above Mrs Strumbold's head. The second gate, leading out of the churchyard, was difficult to negotiate. Not only had it gone under the surface, but there was a shadow across it from a yew tree. I was horribly afraid of running into it and damaging the old woman's legs, which looked as brittle as two sticks of barley sugar. I imagined her falling to pieces like a lay figure, spilling out of the chair as we went along, strewing the path to The Nook with here a foot and there a knee, a shoulder, eyeballs, ears, two or three fingers, a handkerchief, a breast, the wig and valuables she wore on a string round her neck. All these objects, I thought, would be uniformly hard and dry, like so many twigs, acorns, straws, bits of cardboard and rags impregnated with glue.

'Madam,' I resumed urgently, in order to distract myself with calmer and more normal reflections, 'don't give way to depression in this manner. Life is not over at ninety-one. You've often said so yourself and I believe it, fervently. We'll get out our library before going to bed. You always say it makes you sleep better. I'll read your favourite chapters. We'll comment on the pictures. I'm sure it'll be one of your inspired evenings. Do you remember the last time? How we laughed and laughed until we were afraid the neighbours would hear. Oh, if Nancy had only had your wonderful sense of humour. Though I loved her lack of it, naturally. Her seriousness had a piquancy I shall never forget. But that's neither here nor there. We can drink to her health and substitute her name in some of the chapters we read. I wonder what the Swede's called. Not that it matters. We can give him a name — Gustav, Hakon, Sven, what does it signify as long as it's more or less

172

Scandinavian? Mrs Strumbold! Mrs Strumbold!' I exclaimed from the depths of an extraordinary tiredness. 'I doubt if I can stand much more of this without repercussions on my nervous system. Give me a sign. Tell me my fears are unfounded. Insult me. Snore at me. Anything.'

We were now nearing the gate of The Nook. The path ran between hedges and was filled with mist as high as my chin. I walked on tiptoe, sometimes pushing hard and fast, sometimes barely moving. I could not decide which was the best course. Once I stopped and looked back towards the river. I could see only the upper part of the church riding, blue-grey, on a white sea. The yews round it were rocks, laid in the surf of a likely beach. Would we sink together, or would one of us survive?

'Grandma,' I said frantically, 'remember your duty to the younger generation. It's a mistake and a presumption to suppose that you can ever consider yourself alone, even at your venerable age. Oh, my God, why did I ever think it was Nancy whom I loved? I used her as a means of entry into The Nook. I drove her out to find a Swede, or Finn, or anyone she fancied. Why should I care? I wooed you with cooking and dirty books since other advances were not possible. I see it now. What made me imagine it was all done to oblige Nancy? To make the days easier for her and lift the burdens you delighted to load on her back? You have been a witch in your time, Mrs Strumbold.'

We were at the door of the shed where the wheelchair lived. There was a torch on a nail under the window. Though black dark, it was not very misty inside. I had a great disinclination to go further and, especially, to take that cold cylinder in my hand and press the switch near its head. I did not know how I should ever summon the strength to move another step forward.

173

'Listen, listen,' I babbled at tremendous speed. 'I'm ready for anything. I'll dress up in the wigs and evening gowns. I'll put on the high-heeled shoes and twirl the parasol. I'm ready to paint myself all the colours of the rainbow and sing your songs in a falsetto voice. Don't think I've refused in the past out of false modesty. It was just that I wondered whether it was entirely wise. I mean, these antics lead on to others one had not envisaged to begin with. But my doubts have fled. I've no scruples left. All I want is your applause. Your approbation. You.'

I could not detect the smallest movement in the chair, though I leaned hard on the handle and listened as if I'd never heard a sound in the world before. As if my ears were only opened now.

20

JOSEPH clutched his hair and leaned his head far down over his knees. Was this the way Mrs Strumbold had died, or not? 'What if it all happened quite differently?' he muttered in an undertone. 'In any case, I must have got the day wrong. It's impossible that I could have received the news from Nancy, taken the oracle at Swedo-Zero and wheeled Mrs Strumbold into that shed within a space of fifteen hours. There's something missing. Many events must have occurred between these vast happenings. I've telescoped them. Oh-oh!'

He had cruelly twisted both his ears. Supposing everything I've written with such great labour turns out to be a lie, he thought. Perhaps I've slanted the story in the interests of literary composition, dramatic effect, and in order to make it the right length for publication. These ideas depressed him very much. For they seemed to demonstrate that it was scarcely possible to approach the truth, except in an allegorical sense.

Yet, perhaps it was not really so. It might be simply that his difficulties were due to overwork. He could not remember how long he had been incarcerated here, pen in hand. The most sensible course would be to take a complete holiday and then finish the task in one concentrated burst of energy. Yes, on returning from Rome, Paris, Valparaiso, or wherever he finally decided to go, he would be plump, brown and full of beans. Why, he looked like a corpse in the mirror: so cadaverous, such lines of fatigue drawn in a network all over his face. He might be eighty or ninety. His head trembled, his eyelids twitched and his shoulders seemed to have shrunk together under the grey-black pullover.

'Help!' he cried suddenly. But there was no answer except the rhythmic throbbing with which the house resounded. This noise, not loud but most insistent, was located mainly in the walls, as far as he could tell. When he leaned against them he felt it like an electric impulse running through his bones. Sometimes he could hear the papers in the rooms underneath crackling faintly. Once he had rushed down and, after opening the door with inexplicable difficulty, had found a large number of the documents curled at the edges in a curious manner. The trouble was that if he hoped to get to the bottom of the matter, he would have to settle down in those rooms and search until he came on the relevant letters, postcards, contemporary notes and diaries. Perhaps it would be better to postpone such long and taxing research until after the trip to Valparaiso. The change of air would rejuvenate him, he felt certain of it. His old courage in the face of adversity would return to him and he would be able to fling all the doors wide open, turn on the lights and discover what was really there.

Much of it would prove to be rubbish. He was confident of that. Thanks to the sea breezes of Valparaiso, he would easily have the strength to carry great masses of stuff into the garden and set it alight. The smoke would rise to enormous heights, though the flames would not be unmanageable, on account of the damp in the walls, floors and even ceilings. One could smell wet plaster, paper, upholstery, carpets, curtains, all over the house; and that was what chiefly made the crackling of the papers so unnatural.

It proved them to be activated by an outside agency. But a trip abroad, whether to Valparaiso or some nearer place, would enable him to tackle the problem scientifically. His difficulties probably stemmed from his being too artistic and intuitive. If he were to lay in squared paper and make graphs of different sorts, many aspects of his present life would take on a new and clearer pattern.

So the only question now to be settled was whether the cheapness of a sojourn at Valparaiso would compensate for the expense of getting there. Or whether it would, in the end, come to a more modest sum if he were to visit Paris. Of course, France and Italy would provide a greater intellectual stimulus, but there was something romantic and poetic about the name Valparaiso that drew him irresistibly. He did not think that he would ever be able to resolve this problem to his entire satisfaction. Suppose he were to ring up the local travel agency as a first step?

It was a considerable relief, on looking at the window, to see that it was black dark, like the middle of the night, though, naturally, at this time of the year, one couldn't swear that it was more than five o'clock. His watch said two. It was ticking, but had he set it correctly when winding it last? He could not remember. He might ring up and ask the operator the time, but that would mean descending into the hall, below the surface of the manuscripts, which were six feet high in all the rooms, as far as he recollected. He felt very cold at the thought. It had become a great effort to order, and then to fetch from the front door steps, the weekly box of groceries. It took hours to summon enough resolution. Often he gabbled the list of his requirements so fast and so loud that the young lady at the other end became confused, cross, contemptuous, impatient, incredulous and, finally, downright rude. She seldom wrote what he had intended to order and the deliveries were full of surprises, such as perfumed washing-up powder, plastic clothes pegs and poisonous-looking soft drinks. These goods added to the confusion in the house.

But what had Valparaiso to do with all this? He could not imagine how such an extraneous idea had lodged in his head. It almost seemed as if it must have been put there by somebody else. 'Be that as it may,' he whispered, 'I shall not succumb. I feel very strong, really. My health is excellent, in spite of irregular food and no exercise. The amount of work I have done is perfectly enormous. Anyone would look tired in the circumstances. Besides, electric light is not flattering when it comes from one bulb directly overhead. The smallest undulation on the face is magnified and casts a disproportionate shadow. It is necessary to remember also that this mirror is tarnished. It has brown patches and smeary parts. I believe it would give the most beautiful woman a frightening reflection.'

On reaching these conclusions, he smiled with satisfaction, as if obstacles had been cleared out of his way. He would dismiss all thought of Valparaiso, Timbuctoo and various South Sea islands, the names of which had occurred to him of their own volition, suddenly speaking in his head with seductive voices, as though promising freedom and a new sort of happiness. But it would be quite wrong to listen to that kind of thing. His place was here in The Nook. He had been certain of it for many years. Otherwise, he would have moved. What could have prevented him?

He took a sultana cake from under the bed and began to eat hungrily, gnawing at it like a rat, for lack of a knife. Were the tooth-marks on the other side his or not? It was difficult to tell whether such crumbly material had been attacked by pointed rodent teeth, or by the flatter human variety. Certainly the cake was extremely stale and must have been lying about for a week at least. As he swallowed sultanas, currants, nuts, candied peel and small pieces of ginger, his strength returned, together with a distinct sensation of courage. He wondered why he had suffered such terrors of late, starting up in the hope of catching them; trying to lull them into a false security by an appearance of sleep; even shamming death so that they might be encouraged to discover themselves. He was convinced that they would not be able to resist the pleasure of gathering round his body in triumph. Nothing had had the least effect.

But now he was rejuvenated. He sprang up and crammed his glasses on to his nose. He began rummaging on his table for the documents on which he had based the last two chapters. When he had found them, he would check them against what he had written, sentence by sentence. For the whole point of his present trials was that truth should result. If any fictional aspects had crept into his narrative — it was impossible to imagine how this could have happened — he would spot them at once and ruthlessly obliterate offending paragraphs and phrases, even though, from the point of view of art, they might be striking.

Papers slid under his busy fingers which flicked them left and right like a conjuror. Some had dirty creases on them from long folding. Some had lost corners; were long as scrolls; or very small and contained a great deal of minuscule writing; or broad and thick with scattered exclamations. These were not what he looked for. Many appeared to be in another hand, though he couldn't swear to it without a fuller examination.

A loud hammering came from the shelves by the fireplace. There didn't seem to be any particular tune in it, though the notes varied from time to time. He felt slightly hypnotized, and swayed. This impeded his search to a certain extent, as he was obliged to hold on to the mantelpiece with one hand. Opening a small box with difficulty, he extracted a bundle of letters and postcards. All had been sent from the Epsom district, a part of the country quite unknown to him, though not very distant. He supposed it must be a matter of thirty miles, or so, picking one's way through streets with flowering trees planted along the pavement; and dingy streets full of tattered shops and cafés and dismal halls where religious meetings and whist drives were held. One would pass roundabouts, stations covered in years of smoke and caverns full of idle buses. He had often dwelt on this pilgrimage, especially on receipt of a new letter or postcard.

'Have met an amazing Arab prince,' said the one he happened to hold between his nails. 'He's rich and smells of scent which he pours over his hair every morning. Some of it drips on the floor. Lovely.' He read these words with the greatest astonishment. They threw a different light on everything. If only the humming was not quite so loud, he would be able to take a comprehensive view and see where this particular item fitted. He thought now that he could just detect a kind of muted screech under the humming which reminded him of wind in telephone wires.

'Why don't you come?' the next missive complained. 'My prince wouldn't mind. He's a sweet boy. I'd like you to tell them here that I can't eat any more cabbage. The smell of it makes me feel giddy.'

Joseph rested on the back of the sofa, endeavouring to remember how long that box had been on those shelves. A sense of puzzlement drifted over him like a mist. I don't believe my darling was ever in a lunatic asylum, he thought in the end. If she had been, I'd have taken steps of some sort. No, the explanation is much less dramatic. She shared a flat at Epsom with the Swede, the Arab, the American, the Chinaman. Naturally, I never tried to go there. What kind of a welcome would I have received from such a difficult assortment of boys? I could not even have hoped that they would look up to me as the writer of my generation, because they were evidently quite illiterate. Not that I had any definite information as to their intellectual gifts, but it's usually possible for a sensitive man to read between the lines. Take this, for instance: 'Hercules P. Grobleberger has the largest biceps I ever saw in my life. He seldom speaks. I fell under the table with giddiness yesterday, on account of the cabbage. If you were any good, you'd save me.'

'What could I have done for you, dearest?' cried Joseph in a loud voice which did not make the smallest impression on the humming, hammering, screeching, shuffling that pervaded the house. There was also a sensation of people talking under their breath on the landing, but he did not open the door. He remained fixed in front of the mirror, his eyes wide open in a dead-white face. 'Suppose I'd come to Epsom — a town as strange to me as Valparaiso — how could I have persuaded them to change the menus? I had no authority. Questions would have been asked. I might not have given the right answers. What then? They would have detained me. Your communications, sparse though they were, convinced me of that. The repeated references to cabbage proved it beyond doubt.'

He sat down suddenly, the box in his hands, and began feverishly burrowing amongst bundles of paper covered with finger marks and the general scum of reading and re-reading, folding and unfolding, pressing, arranging, cramming into a space too narrow for comfort. Several of the handwritings were unknown to him. There was a torn sheet headed, Dialogue with Mrs Strumbold:

'It's a great mistake to suffer pangs of conscience if it can be avoided. I've known people who became quite incapacitated by the memory of injustices they thought they had done to persons who trusted in them. Wives, for instance, mothers, sisters, tiresome aunts. These actions preyed on them, even though apparently justified by circumstances. Why suffer if it can be avoided? I'm against it at all events. I don't believe it does one good, or teaches one sublime truths. On the contrary, one is merely reduced to a despicable rag. Now that the matron says she's more or less reasonable, ought I to go to Epsom?'

'What for? You don't want her back. Nor do I. She's a drag. I believe you've been at this bottle.'

'No, I swear it. Let me pour for you. I've a feeling I should make a gesture.'

'Oh, a gesture! If that's all you want, please yourself. Do put on the Swedish wig. It suits you. Why isn't there any more cheese sauce?'

'Because you've eaten it. You know, I believe I am improved by blond curls. Shall I do the African dance?'

'Ah!'

'We won't worry about Epsom, then? Huff-puff? Let her stew at Epsom with the shadowy Swede, American, Chinaman, Arab? Ha-huh, I'm getting short of breath, though hardly middle-aged. We'll wait for the matron's next letter before deciding what to do. One doesn't want to rush these things and regret it afterwards. Oh, Mrs Strumb —'

At this point, the page was torn. He threw it on the floor and turned the box upside down on the sofa. Here was another sheet. It was not consecutive, but seemed to bear on the same subject: 'My new book is to be serialized with sensational headings invented by the editor. I'm rather worried about the vulgarity of it, but how can I protest when they pay so much?'

'You can't.'

'I've had news that it's to be translated into Finnish. Imagine the Finns in their perpetual night and snow reading of you and me and Nancy! It's lovely to think of and suggests themes and variations. I might set the next book in perpetual night. I believe it would heighten the effect without seeming too artificial. One wants to avoid being bogged down in symbolism at all costs. I do think, madam, that you might try and keep awake a little longer. It would show not only a degree of politeness, but also gratitude for the electric blanket you are wearing at this moment; the curiously illustrated encyclopedia you have on your lap; the huge cleaning bills I have paid on wigs, gowns, coats with fur collars, hats, gloves, parasols. I don't speak of the very peculiar manner in which I was regarded by the manageress at the cleaners.'

'Why don't you?'

'I prefer not to. Some memories are painful. One doesn't know what to do about them. Suppose I had gone to Epsom, what could I have done except endure a melancholy experience to no purpose? She didn't want to see me. The matron said so. But surely that Swede was as much to blame for her state of mind as I? He deserted her when his studies ended, just like that. Without a second thought. Then there were the American, Arab and Chinaman. Are we to assume that they existed or not? For my part, Mrs Strumbold, I'm inclined to doubt it. I don't altogether believe in the Swede, either. Not after what I saw in that underground club of which I'm certain he was a member. No, madam, let us not be carried away by sentiment, false pity, or general claptrap. Let us keep our heads and take an extended view of the phenomenal world. She was found wandering the streets, singing, dancing and abusing passers-by under various appellations such as: Joseph, Joey-boy,

Jehoshophat, Flatty-platt, Platto, etc. Wasn't that the report we had?'

'Of course it was. Her mother was just the same. Ended up in a place near Dover, as far as I remember. Or it may have been Plymouth. It's so long ago. Some port anyway. The idea was it would be convenient for visiting, but I never went. Poor Mr Strumbold had plans for living near the sea in his retirement. He never lived to retire. Eaten by a shark.'

'Listen to me, for God's sake! What was the point of my trying to visit her while she was in that hostile frame of mind? It would have done no good. The matron admitted it when I questioned her, closely, exhaustively, on the telephone, and by letter, postcard, telegram and special messenger. I did everything possible in the circumstances. My only fear was that I might make her worse by some tactlessness, such as appearing in person, or seeming to reproach her with the suffering she had caused me. I beg you to believe that these were my reasons. Because they were. What motive could I have for deceiving myself? Tell me that. Explain to me.'

Joseph looked down at the sheet of paper he held in his left hand and saw that it was blank. Not a thing was written on it, back or front. Where then could he have got all those words from? He had heard them so plainly. Mrs Strumbold's particular accent still lingered in his ears. She had had a way of spitting out her s's and swallowing her t's which gave her utterance a special quality. Very individual and not to be mistaken even by persons much exhausted by overwork, worry and the enormous strain of speaking the truth without exaggeration, perversion, or other fancy flights calculated to increase the verisimiltude of what they said.

He stared round him as if expecting to see a woman

standing at the door, lying on the bed, bent over the table in a concentrated attitude. The gas fire hissed and the electric light shone down on the top of his head. There were tracks in the dust as though someone had been walking up and down behind the sofa. Marks like snails, or fingers, were traced on the window glass. The air was thick with smoke, whiskey, biscuits, sultana cake and the smell of dirt in all its forms. The furniture, the papers and his hair were equally grey, as if nothing had moved in that room for years on end.

But outside a new era had begun. It was thawing. Lumps of snow fell from the trees and gutters; swathes of it hung over the edges of roofs; the tops of laurel bushes turned green; black puddles appeared everywhere. These changes were invisible, indicated only by the sound of waterfalls and streams which slid down hillocks, walls, balustrades.

21

WHEN the old inhabitants of the town looked out next morning, they saw that there would be a flood in three days' time. Newcomers to the river quarter disbelieved them because many streets were quite a distance from the banks, a thousand yards or so. They did not find it possible to imagine water flowing thigh deep over pavements along which they daily wheeled perambulators. Besides, the river was quite low, at least six feet beneath the esplanade with trees and seats where one sat in summer and watched the boats go past.

To this the old ones doggedly replied that the ground was frozen hard and could not absorb any of the thaw. Great drifts were known to have collected on the hills upstream. Unless the cold weather were to return and slow down the rate of melting, there would be a very deep, bad, terrible flood within three days.

The younger residents remarked that when one got old one became dismal, talking of funerals, disease, sudden death from unexplained causes, flood, hurricane and other disasters. It was only to be expected. Everyone recognized it as a natural development of the human spirit. Marooned in one's house and not able to run out to the shops! Such a current tearing down the road as to make boating dangerous, even for experienced watermen! Ha, ha! These things happened on the films and in America, but not here, not in real life as lived by young couples in ideal

186

homes. Think of the damage it would cause, not to speak of the inconvenience. Obviously, the river board, the town council and the local MP between them would prevent it. These were modern times, full of scientific wonders and technological know-how.

This show of reasoning did not impress the old inhabitants. Three days would demonstrate who was right. They were ready to bet any sum. Sensible people would lay in boats, tins of food and rubber boots. As most craft were now motor driven and therefore unsuited to navigation over fences, bushes, garden seats, doorsteps. and so on, it was advisable to hurry immediately to the boathouses and hire what few punts and skiffs they had.

The new householders remarked patiently that it was nice to see the last of the snow. Tobogganing and skating had been fine, especially for the children, but one had had enough. The coal bills were frightening. One longed for the spring. Once the burst pipes had been mended and all that filthy slush had disappeared, everyone would feel better, even the jeremiahs.

Joseph woke out of a terrible nightmare late on the first day of the thaw. He had dreamed that Mrs Strumbold was bending over him, gripping a knife and fork as he lay, spellbound, on the sofa. He could not move and she was going to start on him immediately, because she happened to be very hungry. Sweat ran down the lines of his face, tunnelling through dirt, collecting coldly on his ragged collar. However, he was now able to understand that it had only been a dream, brought on by lying too long in an awkward position and stimulated, perhaps, by some chance noise outside that resembled the rattling of cutlery held in palsied hands.

He rubbed a spyhole in the window-glass, which was streaming with a damp mist. To his surprise, all the trees, bushes, gates, fences and also the surface of the road, were dark and wet. The mounds of snow cleared from paths were toppling, shrinking, sliding, dissolving. There would be a flood within three days, possibly less. He did not know when this melting had begun. He might have been asleep for days. He ought to go downstairs at once and telephone for provisions of every sort in large quantities. The flood would be long and deep. Even a madman could see that. He observed nothing which would cause a dreamer to find himself stretched on a plate in front of a cannibal.

Yet, he sensed that the house was surrounded. Many invisible people were creeping towards it. Their footprints did now show because the slush was pitted, uneven and covered by an inch of water. One could not trace their advance except by intuition.

'Wait!' he called in a feeble voice. 'I have not said everything. No, no. Not in the least. Permit me to offer my last explanations in full. How can there be rules against that? Truth must be revealed. That is the purpose of my bondage. I have a little notebook here. I laid it ready yesterday, or the day before. Does it matter which? Let us not be too punctilious. It gives such a fussy air to fundamentals. Oh, madam, there has never been any superficial aspect of my life. I've tried to laugh and be amusing, because it's expected, you know. People think it's good to relax. But they're wrong, totally and absolutely wrong. Time is too short and too elusive. Years vanish without one knowing how it happened. What's to be done?'

He fluttered the notebook, trying to find the right place. It had a black grained cover and inside were printed titbits of information: the phases of the moon; lighting-up time; the population of the United States; a ready reckoner for calculating income tax at three and fourpence halfpenny in the pound; the dates of famous battles.

'Thermopylae, Trafalgar,' he muttered in a daze. 'No, that's not what I want; I mean, not at the moment when the waters are rising at a fearful rate. I must make a grocer's list. Masses of tins which can be heated on the gas ring here if the kitchen should go under. What was I looking for in all these pages of writing? The words are joined together in strings from line to line. Is it my hand? I never wrote so closely, in case corrections should be needed. Nevertheless, I believe the key to everything is contained in this book. How worn and fingered it is, as if read and re-read by multitudes of people. One can almost see the tracks of eyes passing through the letters like an express train. Does it matter where I start?' A very ironical face confronted him in the mirror. For a moment, he did not know who it was.

He advanced on the reflection with an ingratiating smile, saying: 'Listen! I have surprising news. Everything you've heard so far is an absolute lie. I have proof of it here. These pages throw new light, new shadow, give new depth and whatever else is necessary to demonstrate the utter superiority of what I now say. Disregard all previous statements. They were exacted under duress. I'm not prepared to explain how it happened in detail. It's too late. Just bear in mind that it was so and has been for a long time, perhaps for years. I don't know. I've had no means of counting, except by the gradual increase of newspapers in the house. There are now so many that it's possible to make only a rough guess at their number.'

He opened the notebook, flattening it on the mantelpiece and, with a delighted grin, began to read: We heard that the Swede had been obliged to call the police because my darling persistently threatened him with a knife and fork, sometimes in the middle of the night when, being drowsy, he was not well able to defend himself. He deposed that she had once nearly carved out his right eye and twice begun sawing his thumbs. He said that though he loved her, in a way, it was too much for any man to bear. It deprived him of his sleep and rendered him unfit for work the next day. He was a zoological assistant by profession and none of his experiences with tigers, pumas, rhinoceroses, elephants, equalled those he had with my darling. In his opinion, she ought to be restrained in a place of safety until she could be persuaded to change her habits. He did not know how this could be done, as she was very resistant to outside influence. He had never been able to effect the smallest change in any of her views. He had tried treating her like an animal and also like a human being with similar lack of success.

These facts I learned on subsequent visits to Swedo-Zero, of which he was a founding member, as I had suspected from the beginning. I would have liked to meet him there and have a discussion over a plate of the onions that appeared to be the only food supplied. It is not a vegetable I care for, but I was prepared for any sacrifice in my darling's interest. I was never lucky enough to catch him, however, for his hours at the zoo were irregular, on account of feeding-times, nocturnal, or semi-nocturnal, habits, birth, death, cleaning out cages and ponds etc. No member of Swedo-Zero could advise me, I found, as to what was the most likely moment to expect him. This was a great grief to me. I cannot express how I longed for first-hand news of my darling.

Eventually, we received a letter from the Epsom district, informing us that my darling was suffering from a pronounced disturbance, but that we ought not to worry because there were now many methods of treating this state of mind. Mrs Strumbold said it had not occurred to her to worry. She was happy to leave everything to the competent authority and to await the outcome with patience. She advised me to do the same. I could appreciate the force of her arguments, yet still felt upset because there seemed to be absolutely nothing I could do to help my darling in her extremity. Mrs Strumbold said she doubted strongly that mad women suffered as much as I supposed, pointing out that they were, in a manner of speaking, unconscious, something like stewed carrots, onions, potatoes or leeks. I remained unconvinced and actually cried a little in the privacy of my bedroom.

Let it not be said that I abandoned my love to the care of government servants. I wrote her many letters, in spite of the fact that I never received any reply. I was careful to inform her of my increasing literary success and of Mrs Strumbold's gradual decrepitude. The old woman became more and more capricious. It must have been at about this date that she began insisting that I took her out in her chair after dark. Perhaps it was a form of vanity on her part. She was very conscious of the deterioration in her appearance since the days when she had been the toast of the tennis club in Singapore. They had even had a photograph of her over the bar, she told me in a burst of confidence once night as we trundled through the churchyard in the mist. I reported these items to my darling, together with extracts from favourable reviews, which I hoped would help to raise her from her melancholy condition.

At this point, he was interrupted by shouts and stones against the window. It was twilight, but he could just discern a figure on the path below. It was gesticulating. Perhaps the message he had waited for so long had come. He wondered whether the caller was a man or woman. Now that everyone wore trousers and padded jackets, it was difficult to tell in the semi-dark. He hoped it was a woman and leaned out saying, 'Yes?'

'There isn't 'alf going to be a flood,' yelled Toby the grocer's man. 'Three feet that river's rose in twelve hours and it's thawing worse than ever. Yeah, day after termorrer we'll be swimming. Them in the new 'ouses don't believe it. " 'Ow can you credit such a thing, Toby," they says, "it's not natural. You think we're going to buy all them extra tins just so's you can get your rake-off," they says. "Why, my 'ubby'll be livid if I do. But Mr Platt. Oy, Mr Platt! 'Ang on. Don't shut the winder. The water's coming. You knows it as well as I does. You been 'ere even longer." So I brought a box what'll last you and any friends you may 'ave staying a good ten days. Yeah, there's prawns, peas, beans, steak, butter, eggs, milk, biscuits, bacon, drink, spaghetti, coffee, tea, verbena soap and I don't know what else. I reminded the manager you must 'ave forgot to ring up and 'e said, Well 'is credit's good enough, better send 'im plenty. Don't want no corpses on our 'ands...." '

'Thanks,' said Joseph. 'I'm much obliged to you for your kindness. I had intended to ring up this afternoon, but it slipped my memory.'

'Yeah,' screamed Toby, beside himself with excitement, 'that's what I said to the boss. Don't forget Mr Platt, I says, because 'e won't remember for a dead cert. 'E's that absorbed in them books of 'is 'e'd be washed away before 'e noticed anythink. 'E's a bookworm, 'e is.'

The window shut suddenly and he remained with his head thrown back and his mouth open. No further sound came from the house, but he thought he could detect vague movements in the rooms where the lights were not on, as if white forms were passing in and out on secret business. He shivered with delight. The place was full of women. One could not doubt it. He waited for a long time, concealing himself behind an adjacent tree. But Joseph did not open the front door to take in the groceries, thus affording Toby a view of the hall and stairs, with women coming down them in a state of undress, to help him lift the awkward, heavy box.

Joseph was standing at the banisters, looking into the darkness from which a distinct sound of pens on gritty paper came. There were at least two hard at work, he judged. They did not hesitate, or cross out, writing at a steady pace from line to line, transferring on to new sheets with a slight rustle.

22

THE third day of the thaw brought great activity to the
river quarter of the town. The weirs were fully drawn, yet
the water did not show the least sign of going down. A mass
of foam, sticks, leaves, tins, bottles, boards and other rubbish swirled past the seats on the esplanade at eight miles
an hour and one inch below the road. It was reported that
there were still vast drifts on the hills. Barely a third of
them had melted. It was also said that everything had gone
and the ground was quite bare and levels falling rapidly
upstream. Some declared that several weirs were blocked
by floating trees which the lock-keepers could not move
because of the pressure of the current through the sluices.
This state of affairs greatly impeded the flow, preventing
millions of gallons of unwanted water from escaping to the
sea. Others said these were rumours put about by shop
managers with the object of frightening people into buying enormous quantities of tinned foods. In this way, they
would be able to sell all sorts of old stuff on the point of
going bad. The authorities should take steps to end the
scandal, prosecuting the grocers for conspiracy and fraud
and sending machinery to deal with the trees, if there were
any. If they did not take these obvious steps, it showed they
were corrupt, in league with the shopkeepers and unworthy of their positions on the council from which they
should be voted at the earliest opportunity.

Others considered that it was not so much dishonesty as

stupidity that was at the root of the menace now moving on the town. If those councillors had had any brains, they'd have realized the snow was bound to melt. The weirs should have been drawn long ago and the stream kept down below summer level. It ought to have been drained off so that the sandbanks between the islands rose above the surface, as sometimes happened during droughts. Why, they should have gone even further and reduced the flow to disconnected puddles. No one wanted to navigate in midwinter. Then there would have been plenty of room for all this appalling water at least to take itself past their homes.

The old inhabitants did not engage in these discussions. They knew there was not time. Coal was delivered to them and those whose sheds might be submerged had it pitched beside the back door. They cleared the shops of boots and waders. Their larders were stacked to the ceiling. Boats were trolleyed into their gardens and tied to stakes they had hammered into the ground at the front door. They arranged parking for their cars at garages in the upper town. For hours on end, they struggled up narrow staircases with chairs, sofas, desks, tables, wirelesses, television cabinets, books, carpets. The cooking stoves they had for summer holidays were laid ready on their landings with pieces of metal under them, in case the gas and electricity failed. They had paraffin, money, magazines, drink, stamps, writing paper, candles and sets of prearranged signals with the neighbours, should it become necessary to attract their attention in an emergency. They opened their gates wide, for once the water was up it would be almost impossible to move them, standing in a boat swept by cross-currents.

When they had done all these things, covered with dirt and sweat as they were, the old hands went to the nearest public house and drank. Some became immensely gay and sang sea shanties. Others related long stories of old ladies and children who had been carried away and drowned; or been marooned in garrets and later discovered dead of starvation. Although their listeners from the new estates didn't believe a word of it, seeing how drunk they were, yet a horrible cold feeling spread over them and they did not know what to think, huddling together at one end of the bar and trying to laugh.

Joseph knew that all these things were happening. He ought to have cleared the downstairs rooms. In a moderately bad flood, the water did not rise above the top step outside the door. But one glance down the road, where even the marks of snow had disappeared, told him this was going to be a tremendous inundation. The carpets down there would be ruined. So would the furniture. He was not worried about them. He had no use for them and, in any case, they were in rags and splinters, as far as could be seen through the layers of dust and paper by which they were concealed. His dereliction of duty concerned the manuscripts.

Many were very faintly written and it was by no means certain that they would be legible afterwards when they had been dried. Besides, imagine the enormous labour of drying them, sheet by sheet! Pad by pad! Notebook by notebook! The most modern machines would be necessary if one hoped to perform such a task within one's lifetime. It might take decades, the machines whirling sixteen hours a day, to overcome the effect of present neglect.

And that was not the sum. Far from it. The pages would be indelibly water-marked, brown streaks and stains wandering over the writing and making it even more difficult to decipher, if that were possible. The edges would be curled, unless one were to embark on the superhuman task of ironing every single document, the iron at precisely the right temperature and the paper with the right amount of moisture still remaining to prevent scorching. Plainly that was out of the question. The edges would remain cockled in all directions.

That would not seem to matter, at first sight. He was no stickler for neatness. It had never been his habit to go round straightening rugs and cushions and wiping the dust off shelves. No, the consequences he envisaged were quite other and far more dreadful. Each page, if not flat, would take up twice as much room as before. The manuscripts would thus advance up the stairs in a concentrated rush. They would fill the two spare bedrooms in a trice. Who could say that these would be enough for them? It required a computer to give a steady answer to such a question. Only an inhuman intelligence could face the horror of it. That was why he remained here, flat on his bed, as if glued to the mattress, his eyes turned up.

But he must not despair. It should be remembered that many of the papers were both old and of poor quality. It might be that three or four days' submersion — or even a week with luck — would dissolve them completely. They might become an abominable mash on the floor which could be swept into the garden with a stiff broom. He had only to beckon the Qwikcleen representative as he went whistling past in order to be supplied with any number of brooms, brushes, dustpans, shovels, buckets, sponges and mops. He imagined the scene with a disbelieving sigh. All the manuscripts become an indecipherable porridge and himself shovelling and brushing them into a heap, pouring paraffin on them and striking matches. He would do it after dark and the blaze would be visible for miles around.

Had he, then, decided to leave them to soak and thus defeat the malignant influences which had their habitation mainly in the lower storey, though the landing was by no means clear? One had only to step on to it to discover that. The banisters thrummed and a kind of effluvium that might have been concentrated breath, rose from below. How was he to complete his masterpiece under these circumstances? How capture the truth that was the object of his being, the only reason why he did not simply march down into those rooms and allow himself to be suffocated?

As he cogitated thus, the high-pitched cries of Moslem dustmen sounded faintly. The corporation had ordered garbage to be cleared from the entire river quarter of the town. When the bins were empty, experienced inhabitants sallied out with bits of rope and tied them to the nearest upright, to prevent their floating off. One could plainly hear the crash of planks being thrown out of lorries. These were for the catwalks to be erected across the shallow and more sheltered parts where the currents would not be strong enough to wash away the supports. Red lanterns were festooned on them at night. They were invariably wet and wobbly, so that many people, and even dogs, fell off them and caught their death of cold, if elderly.

'Notwithstanding all this,' thought Joseph, 'I must get up. I must make an effort. It's now or never.' He remained supine because he was so tired, which was natural in the circumstances; no one could deny it. The immense box of groceries lay on the doorstep like bait in a trap. How was it to be got upstairs to the comparative safety of this room? That had been his problem and he had struggled to solve it for a long time, occasionally poking his head out of the window, or door, but mostly sitting bolt upright on the sofa with his ears cocked for footsteps. These he had heard at irregular intervals and still did.

They seemed to belong to two people, as well as he could judge. Busy people who knew their way about and what they wanted to do. It was probable that they were opening cupboards and shifting light objects, such as chairs, small tables, framed photographs, wigs. He formed this opinion from the noises and also from sudden puffs of dust that seemed to travel up to him and could not be caused by draughts as all windows and outside doors below were tightly shut and, indeed, could hardly be opened, in the case of the windows, without the aid of hammers, chisels, screwdrivers and main force.

So he had been obliged to meditate at length as to the best way of retrieving his groceries and also a couple of saucepans, a tin-opener and a selection of cutlery from the kitchen. Once he had got the supplies safely into the room, it was his intention to lock the door and damn the consequences. He had looked forward to that triumphant moment enormously as he stood poised on the top step like a diver. Finally, he had dived. He could congratulate himself on that. He had torn down with cotton wool in his ears, scarcely hearing any sound of pursuit. Rushing into the kitchen like a whirlwind, he had seized the necessary implements without fumbling, flung them on top of the box and got up again, half dead for lack of breath and weakness in the back and legs that seemed to drag him from behind, as though gravity itself were fastened on his coat-tails like a vice.

After securing the door and placing the load of provisions against it, he had lain in a heap on the carpet for an indefinite period. Then he had recovered sufficiently to climb on the bed, unplug his ears and listen. To his astonishment, the manifestations had entirely ceased. It was this which gave him the idea that he ought to do something about the manuscripts, or, at any rate, the most important of them. If he took advantage of the lull, he could salve many essential documents. The presences had been vanquished by surprise tactics. They had never suspected he could summon enough courage to capture the box, disregarding the obvious way in which they were patrolling in the hall, backwards and forwards and cross-ways from room to room. On mature examination, the episode proved them bullies, ready to run for it on the first sign of opposition, of a firm stand on one's rights as a sentient human being. He put one foot on the floor.

Immediately there was a hush; not the ordinary quiet-ness of an empty house. No, no, far intensified. People were standing in mid-step and holding their breath. They were both staring at the corner of the stairs round which he would appear, if he came down. They had made plans during the interregnum. Who could guess what these were? One could certainly assume they were hostile plans without much fear of contradiction. It would be better not to commit oneself to this salvage of the manuscripts too hastily. He drew his foot back on to the bed and filled his ears once more with cotton wool.

'The water! The water! It's coming down the road!' The cry rose thinly on the winter afternoon, percolating into the bars where the old hands shrugged resignedly and ordered another round. Anyone wearing rubber boots, they said, could safely put off his return home for two hours. The people from the new estates did not stay for more advice, rushing out immediately to view the pheno-menon. They had no boots, nor prospects of obtaining any within the next two hours. The shops were sold out. The question of tins agitated them greatly. Of course, their larders contained a good supply, in case people dropped in unannounced for a meal; or they hadn't time to cook on account of appointments, entertainments, or lack of a shil-ling for the meter. But now that this appalling water was rolling down the gutters, they remembered films they had seen of people swept away on tidal waves in a flurry of telegraph poles, roofs, doors, arm-chairs, straw hats. The sound-effects had been tremendous with roaring and thundering and magnified screams.

As they stood debating, the water grew broader. It overflowed the gutters and began trickling into gardens. The crown of the road was like a sandbank. It was still just possible to jump across the stream and arrive home dryshod. Perhaps the most horrible thing was the silence and inexorability of the flood's advance. There was no danger of being suddenly overwhelmed, but what if it would not stop? What if it rose, steadily and peacefully until one was standing on the chimney pots, imploring those who had hired boats to take one up? But these were silly fancies. The corporation would do something. Parliament, the army, the air force, the bishops and the river board would set some wonderful plan in motion, based on the latest principles of science.

Within two hours, the only noises to be heard in the river quarter were wirelesses and the gentle bump of boats swinging on their moorings. The water looked black under the street lamps. The stream was becoming a little faster in places, at cross-roads, for example, and corners where there was a wall. Here the flood murmured very slightly.

Joseph sighed. He had fallen into a half-sleep and dreamed that he got into a dinghy and rowed across a huge expanse of dark water until he came to his publishers, where he was received with the greatest cordiality and all his problems vanished so completely that he could not remember in what they had consisted, even in the most general terms.

23

ON the first morning, the flood was not particularly deep. Anyone with waders could get about quite easily. Boating was not too difficult as the stream was fast only in certain places. Wherever there were hedges and fences to act as breakwaters, it was just like a lake. The sun shone and the many dazzling reflections from ripples, windows and greenhouses was cheerful. Those with boats set out for the newspapers. One could hear their voices and the splash of oars echoing along the streets. Children ran on the cat-walks, bouncing the planks like springboards. Several elderly women complained of such behaviour, which made it impossible to reach a betting shop where they wished to place sixpence each way on a greyhound due to run that evening. This dog was a certain winner. One of the tipsters had declared it. No one took the least notice of what these women said. They lived in an old folk's home near the edge of the flood and were notorious moaners.

Everybody laughed, for it was exciting to have the water just deep enough to make the neighbourhood interesting, yet not so bad as to cause alarm. No one was short of food or coal; or obliged to live upstairs in candlelight; or suffer-ing from rheumatism, bronchitis, deadly chills or stream-ing noses brought on by damp and cold and wet clothes that couldn't be entirely dried, no matter what one did. Those who had been too lazy to drag their furniture and carpets up from the ground floor congratulated themselves on their good sense. Very likely the flood would rise no higher. At the worst, there was at least a foot to spare. Many people could remember times when the water had been actually within half an inch of entering the houses and had miraculously receded. The last occasion this had happened was about fifteen years ago.

Joseph woke late and immediately looked out. The garden was full of water as he expected. The bushes swayed when lorries passed. These were provided by the corporation for the use of citizens cut off in the flood. But as one had to devise some means of getting through one's garden to the road in order to board them, they were most useful to persons who found themselves on one of many temporary islands formed by undulations of the ground and containing two or three houses each. Even they were not always taken up, though they stood shouting and waving their arms, because the lorries were already full of sightseers from outside the district who had taken the opportunity of a free trip round the disaster area, as it was called in the newspapers.

How delightful it would be just to sit here watching the reflections and the passing show, Joseph thought with longing. He would prop himself comfortably with cushions and pillows on the table and listen to the swish of water which could be heard long before anyone came into view. People would call up to him in a friendly way, on account of the emergency, and he would answer, saying he'd plenty of tins, but if anyone was going to his newsagent, he'd be very glad of the papers on their way back. And they, forgetting his terrible reputation and the many times he had snubbed them, would struggle with his gate and punt in and he would let down a basket. The days of the flood would pass like a peaceful dream.

Unfortunately, it was not possible to surrender to this

temptation. The footsteps were on the stairs and he could hear low talking, as if serious consultations were going on. He tried to make out the words, but they mumbled one into the other without any of the pauses for breath a human throat would have to take. Even when he lay on the floor with his ear hard against the crack at the bottom of the door, he could only distinguish sounds resembling, strummm, strumboooo-strummm. It was extraordinary. He was lulled and almost went to sleep, relaxed and curiously warm, in spite of a stiff draught whistling down his neck from the landing.

He jumped to his feet, realizing for the first time that it was their intention to kill him. Since he had refused to descend into their territory, they were invading his. They were standing together just outside. Their plans had been laid and he had not a moment to lose. He must finish this last chapter and then, with the manuscript under his arm, he would throw up the window and scream for help. People would come, scenting a mystery, and he would let himself down into their boat and help them to row away from The Nook for ever. He would flee to his publishers, who would receive him with cordiality on account of past sales and the hints he had given them at intervals during his present labours. He believed he had had a prophetic dream on this subject a short time back.

Yet, could one be sure of anything? Had he really discovered the last adventures of Nancy and her grandma? Was he grieved by their departure, however it had happened? He had a distinct feeling that if they had indeed quitted the world it was in a manner quite different from that described in his colossal work, now covering the table in a compact layer eighteen inches thick. He stared at it in a daze and ruffled the edges here and there. Little round lights reflected from the water outside danced all over the walls and ceiling. Sometimes they came together as if they had news to impart to each other. Sometimes they shivered and shook as if roaring with laughter: heh, heh, heh, huh.

He drew a sheet out from near the bottom and began reading with great surprise. It contained views he had never expressed and was not in his writing. Nor could he swear it was Mrs Strumbold's hand. It seemed to be something between the two. How amazing. He perused the ragged loops and twirls that raced along the lines like one possessed.

'I was, of course, much alarmed by my darling's long incarceration in a state institution. I wrote many letters demanding information from the highest authorities as to her condition. I particularly wished to know what name they had given her illness so that I could look it up in a medical encyclopedia and find out exactly what the symptoms were and whether I myself had ever suffered from them in a mild form. If I had not, I could not be accused of having infected my darling during our association. I explained my motives to the doctor in charge at length, so that he should be under no misapprehension as to their importance. I told him plainly not to shilly-shally because I was the warmest friend Nancy had in this world. To the best of my recollection, I received no answer.

'I wrote again in very civil tones, begging the doctor to have pity on the anxieties under which I laboured as a direct result of his neglectful habits with his correspondence. I pointed out that his secretary, whose wages were shouldered by the taxpayer, could easily be instructed to send me copies of his reports — not necessarily clean ones; I was not fussy on small points. But I felt I must insist on being treated as a responsible member of Nancy's family, since I had been her first and only true lover. I'm glad to say he sent me the following note, here appended.'

Joseph frowned over the crumpled paper attached by the corner with glue to the main sheet. It contained an indecent drawing which he recognized as a copy of an original owned by Mrs Strumbold. How muddling. He must persevere through every discouragement, not allowing himself to be distracted by seeming irrelevancies. Time was horribly short. He could hear impatient feet and a soft sort of knocking, as if with a gloved fist or a foot wearing fur-lined slippers. He reached for the cotton wool and filled his ears.

The flood, which had steadied for some hours, now began to rise again, rippling past the lamp posts at increasing speed, swallowing the bushes in the gardens, creeping up the steps in front of doors. People who had enjoyed watching the lorries full of trippers, newspaper men and television cameras, shivered as they measured the depth, leaning from the windows with stones tied on the end of strings. What would become of those who had no boats when they had eaten everything in the house?

Joseph took another handful of manuscript from a different part of the table. Working on the principle of random samples and opinion polls, he would extricate the essential meaning of what he had written in this first draft. The second redaction would thus be an extremely concentrated statement. That was all that was necessary. Why bother with embroidery? He polished his glasses and began again with renewed ardour.

'I shall never forget the day I opened the letter announcing my darling's recovery. The fog was thick and pressed tightly all round the house. It had got into the hall — through the letter-box, perhaps — and hung under the light as I stood there, transfixed by the news that Miss Strumbold could be fetched from Epsom between the hours of ten and five thirty. I turned the matter over carefully in my mind in order not to be carried away by natural emotion to conclusions, and even actions, that might seem unconsidered in retrospect. I took the pad and pencil from beside the telephone and began writing, for that was the only way I could discover the right course to follow.

'Far be it from me, my dear sir, to lecture on subjects with which you are, alas, only too well acquainted. Forgive my presumption in venturing to address you at all, except on trivialities. It is simply that I have known Miss Strumbold over a period of years. I have studied her character attentively and I can state with confidence that she is a deceptive woman. You may think she is entirely normal. I made the same mistake myself once. Heavens above! I'd no idea she planned to do me in with a knife and fork in the middle of the night. I can assure you, my dear sir, that was a most alarming episode, chiefly because I had no warning. She gave no indication when I left her bedroom that she was shortly going to follow with these weapons I have mentioned. She waited until she thought I would be thoroughly drowsy and unable to react quickly enough to save myself. Not wishing her to be charged with a criminal offence, in addition to her other troubles, I never complained of the injury she did me. I am healthy and heal soon. Don't imagine I'm reluctant to fetch her between ten and five thirty, or any other hours for that matter. It's merely that I want to warn you as a sincere well-wisher. Your reputation as a doctor may be at stake.'

But where did I get this stuff from, Joseph wondered in profound dismay? It is absolutely at variance with the story as hitherto conceived. He stood up and regarded himself in the mirror, calmly and reflectively. Taking the wool out of one ear, he heard a voluptuous sigh and put it back immediately. He would pause in his work, have a snack, recapitulate. He believed he was getting somewhere at last and, if he didn't rush things, might very well bring his task to a long-desired conclusion. Oh, long-awaited, prayed-for, dreamed-of day when he would be free to leave The Nook to fill with water and disintegrate. Hurrah!

He groped under the sofa and drew out a chopper previously concealed there. It was the work of a moment to break a hole in the partition wall between his room and the bathroom, to squeeze through and bolt the other door and barricade it with a chair to make quite sure. He felt triumphant and happy as he filled his saucepan at the tap. He would heat up a tin of spaghetti, collect himself, have a nap. There was time for a short one. He had them at a disadvantage now. They never guessed he'd actually dare to attack their shrine with a hatchet. Maybe he would later have the courage to sally out and drive them down the stairs, through the hall, into the flood. Who knew? He watched the tin bouncing in the boiling water contentedly.

24

EVERY day the flood rose higher and the stream ran faster down the roads. Boxes, branches, chairs, firewood, collected in corners and then suddenly poured over the top of fences and hedges. One could watch them bobbing and twirling into the distance for quite a long time from the upstairs windows. The houses ran with a most penetrating damp. It was like living in a well. Sometimes the water steadied for as long as six hours and people eagerly made marks on their walls, so that if it dropped even by a quarter of an inch, they would know; once it started to fall, it would not rise again. The old inhabitants had said so categorically. But their hopes were always dashed.

It was now too deep for lorries and the corporation had provided a service of punts, which would have been a great comfort and convenience had they not been loaded to sinking point with sightseers, who sailed past shouting with excitement, especially at dusk when lights were on and it was possible to view the stricken families in their upstairs rooms. Helicopters fluttered overhead perpetually taking photographs and making startling reports that were carefully followed on their wirelesses by the people in the water below.

Perhaps the worst thing was the awful boredom of sitting in the middle of the flood day in, day out. How to pass the hours? One did not dare to eat too much, even though the Qwikcleen representative was now travelling in tins. He had got a boat, heaven knew how, and filled it with crates of human food, dog food, bird seed, cat fish and baby food. With the help of Toby to punt at the bow, he penetrated into roads and lanes where the currents were so treacherous that even experienced watermen would have hesitated, for fear of being suddenly swept into the main river and dashed to pieces on the weir. No one knew enough of his background to say where he could have learnt this supreme boating skill.

Joseph was not afflicted by ennui; or fear of starvation; or of the bandits rumoured to be rowing about with muffled oars all night, searching houses where the owners, being rich, had provided themselves with boats, and set course for the nearest hotel. Every minute he could spare from sleep he passed in writing, and reading what he had written. He believed he was at last beginning to make sense of the whole business. Two pens and six pencils, ready sharpened, lay on the mantelpiece. It seemed that the final statement he had sought during all the years of his imprisonment in The Nook was on the very point of appearing. There were moments when he thought that it had actually materialized, but that he had missed it in the confusion of sound and movement in the house; and the situation was now complicated by the thick layer of dirt and plaster on all flat surfaces since his attack on the bathroom wall. One could not decipher the papers without first blowing off them vast clouds of dust, which resettled on neighbouring memoranda, on his hair, spectacles, ears, hands, pen and the bit of paper where he hoped to make supplementary notes. Nevertheless, he persevered. What else could he do?

'I wrote many times to the authorities at Epsom, and also to my darling, as it was not my intention to do anything behind her back. She received copies, suitably abridged, of every communication I had with the doctors in charge of her case. My one fear was that mistakes should be made through ignorance of the special circumstances affecting my darling, myself and Mrs Strumbold. How could commonplace psychiatrists be expected to guess the delicate balances and stresses necessary to keep an artist working to the limit of his capacity? Had they the experience to understand the utter necessity of writing to a writer? I did not wish to cast aspersions on professional men and women. It was my desire to give them the benefit of the doubt wherever possible. Yet, I addressed them substantially as follows.

'I don't know what Miss Strumbold may have told you about me, but you should, in fairness, listen to the other side of the story. I have suffered supremely from that woman's antics. Her turning hot and turning cold, as though one were condemned to spend one's life running round and round the different rooms in a Turkish bath. Dear sir, imagine my position. It so happens that I did, in fact, first meet her outside a Turkish bath for ladies which had recently closed, owing to expiry of the lease. That was how we got into conversation. Would she have captivated me, instantly and completely, in the doorway of a sweet shop, for instance, or a tobacconist's? No, she would not. My whole subsequent career would have been different in that case, but whether for better or for worse I am not competent to say.

'Dear sir, I have for a long time been stuck at a most terrible impasse. I can go neither forward nor backward. You will appreciate that this is a situation which cannot be allowed to continue. It is impeding my work. That is to say, my life. How can such things be permissible? What I mean is that I cannot receive her. She is too disturbing. My books have begun to be successful only since she left. You must keep her. What is one more in your establishment? You won't notice it. She will be submerged. But here, in a small house, face to face, it can't be done. The prospect is unendurable. Writing is done from memories. It's recollection in as much tranquillity as can be mustered by a hard-pressed author. I'm not a wilful egoist. I'm obliged to live the way I do by a character for which I was not, in the first place, responsible. And a nature has its own dynamism. It evolves without one being aware of what is happening. One is presented with a *fait accompli* and it comes eventually to this: I cannot by any means bring myself to communicate further with the Epsom district, or anyone residing in it.

'Dear sir, I am immensely sorry to have to make this statement. I am ashamed of it. Who would wish to appear in a despicable light if it could be avoided? Be that as it may, I appeal to you as a man of the world, as a doctor, as a person of considerable importance whichever way one looks at it. Spare me. Her grandmother has recently died under circumstances that need not concern you. I see my freedom in the balance. Oh, my God, what more can I say to convince you?'

The flood was now tearing down the streets in little waves and whirlpools. Many fences and sheds had collapsed under the pressure and no longer acted as breakwaters round the houses. How long would a wall stand unprotected in a rushing torrent before the bricks and mortar were undermined? No one knew. The river had not been so deep and fast in living memory. There had never before been any danger. One had just sat it out in the bedrooms and cleared up the mess afterwards. People began to see cracks snaking across the downstairs rooms. They heard unusual noises, half-smothered by the eternal sound of water. No one could hope to swim for it. Shouted consultations were held from house to house. The telephone had gone. The gas had gone. The electricity had gone. They screamed these items to each other.

But behold the mayor and corporation sailing against the tide of debris in a procession of motor boats. As they came they shouted through loud hailers that a world-wide distress fund had been launched for the flood victims, on whom the eyes of the whole nation were fastened sympathetically. The navy was coming with amphibious vehicles, landing-craft, rope ladders, life-jackets. Anyone wishing to be evacuated had only to hail them and it would be done. Mattresses and plates of soup were being prepared in the Methodist hall, the town gymnasium and in a council boys' home from which the boys had been temporarily cleared.

Furthermore, the corporation bellowed right and left, the army had been summoned with every kind of equipment for crossing rivers in spate. Their officers would order them to cruise the district with loads of corned beef, bread and tea. Anyone requiring provisions had simply to call. No payment would be asked. Everything possible was being done to succour citizens in difficulties. Let them rest assured. They had not been forgotten by their mayor and corporation. A full-scale publicity campaign had been started and titled persons had been approached for their support.

These messages echoed over the water far and wide and all the people crowding the upstairs windows heard them plainly. They listened intently, hopefully and disbelievingly; as the stentorian voices faded, the procession could no more be seen and drowned hens, cats, and other rubbish darted past their doors.

25

JOSEPH wrote: 'How can one explain when the last
extremity approaches and one's time is done? Dear sir, I
am addressing you from the middle of a dangerous flood,
but that's by the way. It is not the water which I fear. No,
no. Why do I waste attention on such things? I want to
speak of freedom. It's a subject I've pondered with the
greatest assiduity. And you, sir, must have interesting
opinions, considering the numbers of persons you have incarcerated against their will. The mere thought of it appals
me. I understand so well. Don't imagine that I haven't
grieved for my darling in her misfortune. Heavens above,
what sort of a brute do you take me for? You are utterly
mistaken. I would welcome her tomorrow, if circumstances
permitted. I would come with a bouquet between the
hours of ten and five thirty, as laid down in your printed
notice, now before me on my desk.

'But it's impossible, impossible, impossible. I can't start
again, as if we were standing outside the Turkish baths. I
know too much and I've written it all down somewhere.
I know I have. Not only that, but the next chapter also. I
remember distinctly. I described how your letter came, informing me that Miss Strumbold, being now cured, had
left your institution for an undisclosed destination. It was
no part of your duties to keep track of her movements,
once her freedom had been granted by the board of direc-
tors. You need not have been stiff with me. I was merely

enquiring, without the least idea of questioning your decisions. It was just that your vagueness on this subject left me trembling. I was listening all day long for her footsteps and it interfered with my work, which had entered a difficult stage, requiring full concentration.'

Oh, my God, thought Joseph, why am I so long-winded? The facts are short and very succinct, yet I don't seem able to record them on account of the way the door is bulging inwards, as if strong pressure were being exerted on the other side. Surely that crack round the lintel was not there yesterday? The window-sill is crooked. The mirror is falling down. It's all because I can't make up my mind whether my darling hanged herself in the shed at the bottom of the garden or not.

I couldn't state on oath that I went down there to see how Mrs Strumbold's wheelchair was getting on and found her suspended from the rafters. I used to visit the place once a month and consider that chair. The seat and back had rotted away, but the frame was iron. Should I, one night, carry it along the footpath, through the churchyard, and throw it into the river? Should I plant it in a flower bed and buy a climbing rose, or floribunda, guaranteed quick-growing? It's beyond me to express the agony this problem caused. I must have spent months trying to decide. It's a period I can't recall with any exactitude. Did I find her hanging? Did I hang her? How did Mrs Strumbold really die? When was it? Long ago, or just before this flood? A note of these events was certainly made at the time because I'm essentially a methodical man, guided by reason, by a consuming desire for the freedom I have somehow missed. What else is there for me then?

Toby and the salesman came gliding over the flood. With a skilful shove, they turned their punt under the lee of The Nook. It rested just outside the bottom windows.

The rooms were full of water half-way up the walls. Dirty postcards, wigs and women's clothes floated in confusion above the table tops. There was a great crack running across the north-east corner and the ceiling sagged. The neighbours on either side had been evacuated yesterday, but Mr Platt had refused to accompany them, although the rescue people said his house was rapidly becoming unsafe. A whole line of six or eight houses here was being undermined. The rescue people had stared into the downstairs rooms and up at Joseph, while the neighbours told them some story of mysterious deaths, women and amazing domestic activities. But it was all too involved to grasp. They could make nothing of it and went away.

Toby and the salesman now called to Joseph, saying they were his friends and had come for him at considerable personal risk. The Nook was falling down. Let him step into their boat and they would punt him to safety, not asking questions, or expecting him to confide in them more than he wished. They would see to it that he got a room in a hotel. Naturally, he would not be required to bed down in the Methodist hall, cheek by jowl with curious neighbours. They implored him to come.

But Mr Platt seemed only to shake his pen at them angrily — that was if he had noticed them at all. His room was dark except for two candle-ends guttering in saucers. He appeared to be hunting through the pages of a large notebook. It looked as if he had cotton wool in his ears, though they thought afterwards that this must have been a mistake. It was so nonsensical. The place was as quiet as a grave.

They renewed their entreaties, saying that they could not wait for ever. Darkness was coming on and navigation was dangerous when one could not see, on account of the large amount of rubbish floating at tremendous speed; and the many sunken objects, such as cars, bicycles, spiked railings; and the fact that all the street lamps had failed. They said it was unlikely that The Nook would last the night. Did he wish, at his age, to spend the small hours perched on a broken bit of wall, catching his death of cold? The rescue people could not return before dawn.

They said they did not blame him for anything that might have happened in the past. They themselves had never believed any of the stories concerning his private life. Besides, it was no business of theirs. Live and let live was their motto. Censorious attitudes did no good and only interfered with trade. Let him open the window. Let him descend. They could stay no more. Dusk had fallen and the water was running faster than ever. The corners were more tricky to negotiate. The cataracts at the cross-roads required enormous strength in order to keep a loaded punt head on to the current and force one's way over.

Mr Platt had sunk down at his table and was reading the notebook at breakneck speed. They could see him turning the pages one after the other. He had the pen in his teeth. They debated whether to break into the house and drag him out. It would expose them to a charge of assault, if he should turn nasty afterwards, of course. But that was a minor consideration. The real trouble was that he was a raving lunatic. They realized it now. If he struggled in the boat it would founder and they would all be swept away. Was it their duty as citizens and humanitarians to die for his sake?

As they took up their poles and began to push, they thought they saw him laughing wildly, the pen still between his teeth. Whether this hilarity was directed at them, or caused by something in the notebook, they could not determine. Perhaps it had been an illusion, due to the uneven light of the two candle-ends. They argued quite heatedly about this as they fought towards the shore. For they were utterly weary after a whole day on the water.

When the rescue people came at dawn, resolved to seize Mr Platt and stand no nonsense, they found The Nook a tumbled ruin. The side wall had collapsed and the upstairs floor was canted at a steep angle. There were various corners where a man might easily have taken refuge while waiting for help, but they were all empty. An air of such desolation hung over the place that one could not avoid a feeling that no one had ever lived there and Mr Platt had never existed.

Printed by
Northumberland Press Ltd
Gateshead on Tyne